The Travelers Detective Club

SAN FRANCISCO BAY AREA

SUSSI VOAK

DEDICATION

To my community in Oakland, CA and the surrounding Bay Area. I may have moved away, temporarily, but my heart belongs in the Bay.

Table of Contents

1. It Begins Again

Jeremy froze halfway up the stairs to his room. A reporter on the evening news was part way through his monologue. "... disappearance of the Union Square Christmas tree caused panic and confusion this afternoon. Witnesses reported it vanishing around one o'clock. Calls to the ..."

Jeremy didn't wait for the reporter to finish his story. He raced up the remaining steps, flung his door open and grabbed his camera off his desk.

"What's going on?" Thing asked.

Jeremy ignored him. He depressed the power button. "Come on, come on." The camera started up. Jeremy pushed the review button and scanned through his pictures. Hours earlier he'd come back from his class trip to the Exploratorium, which included a detour to

10

Union Square. He'd asked a classmate to take a picture for him while they were standing on the corner, blocks away from the square but with it still in view. Jeremy thought he'd heard several people yell, but his class was three blocks ahead, and he'd had to run to catch up. "Whoa."

"What?" Thing asked from his place on the bed. Thing was a magic buddy, given to Jeremy when he became a member of the Travelers Detective Club.

"Look at these pictures," Jeremy said.

"You mean the ones that show that you didn't bring me with you?"

Jeremy pretended not to hear. He sat down on the bed. "This one has a tree in the background." He held it up for Thing, now standing on his shoulder. "But this one doesn't."

"And you're just noticing this now?" Thing jumped on Jeremy's head. "A smart one, you are."

"Really? Now you're Yoda?" Chuckling, Jeremy grabbed Thing off his head and put him back on the bed. Orange and round, and about the size of a softball, Thing had extremely short arms and big hands, no legs with feet, a tail and hair sticking up on top like a mohawk. He had big beady eyes but no mouth. To an outsider he looked like a stuffed animal design gone wrong.

"Hey, have you been playing with my computer again?" Jeremy sat at his desk, his laptop open.

"Who, me?" Thing's voice reminded Jeremy of one of the Ewoks from Star Wars, only slightly deeper.

"Yes, you. Unless you're not alone up here."

"I get bored. You leave me here all by myself," Thing whined as he jumped off the bed onto the floor.

"I see you went up a level on Pac-Man. You know there are other games that are way more interesting." Jeremy began typing.

"But are the characters as cute as Pac-Man?" Thing crawled up a leg of the chair and onto Jeremy's lap.

"Do they remind you of anyone?" Jeremy asked, pressing send.

"No. Why would they?" Thing said from Jeremy's shoulder.

Smiling, Jeremy waited. Moments later a ringing came from his computer. He clicked the green button on the screen, and before he could say hello, Thing butted in.

"Hey, Devon, where's Birdbrain?"

"Hi, Thing," Devon said. "She's right here."

Birdbrain was Devon's magic buddy: a stuffed bird with ruffled feathers and an oversized beak.

"Not now, Thing. I need to talk to Devon."

"It's always got to be about you," Thing complained. "What about me and Birdbrain, huh? Huh?"

Before Jeremy could reply, Thing leaned into the camera so that his eyes filled the screen. A moment later a close up of Birdbrain's right eye and beak stared back at Jeremy.

Jeremy heard Devon chuckling, as Birdbrain disappeared from view. "Hi, Jeremy. Excited for break?"

"Yeah, listen. The Christmas tree in Union Square in San Francisco disappeared.

"You're kidding."

"No. It was on the news, and I've got pictures on my camera. We had a field trip to San Francisco today."

"Wait. What? How could it have just disappeared? Oh no? You don't think—"

"A Christmas tree?" Thing interrupted. "I didn't know it was a Christmas tree." Thing did a backflip onto Jeremy's head. "Christmas is coming? Yay! Are you getting me something this year?" Jumping back down to Jeremy's shoulder and leaning into the camera's view, Thing added, "Did you know, he has never gotten me a Christmas present." Thing turned and glared at Jeremy.

"Nice view," Birdbrain chuckled. "You know, that tail of yours is … diminutive."

"What? Thanks … wait. What does that even mean?"

"Still studying the thesaurus I see," Jeremy laughed.

"Will someone please tell me what that means," Thing demanded.

"She thinks you have a cute tail," Devon said.

"That's not—" Birdbrain started, but Devon shushed her.

"Do you think it's the man from Paris, the one who stole the magic hat?" Devon asked while repeatedly nudging Birdbrain away from the screen. "Birdbrain, will you please stop."

"Ffffttt."

"Way to tell her," Thing said to Birdbrain.

Trying to ignore Thing, flipping from his shoulder to his head and back again, Jeremy said, "That's what I was thinking. It sounds just like Paris all over again." He caught Thing midflip, and tossed him on the bed. "But why would he come all the way here?"

"Maybe he wanted to get out of Europe," Devon said, "try his magic elsewhere, maybe get away from us. Wait. Did he think we were all from Paris?" Addie, a TDC member they'd met in Paris, was French. Devon, however, lived in Portland, Oregon while Jeremy was from Oakland, California.

Thing paused mid jumping jack. "How could he confuse Birdbrain and me with that stuffy horse?" he said, referring to Napoleon, Addie's magic buddy. Meanwhile, Thing's gymnastics baffled Jeremy. Something seemed wrong with Thing doing jumping jacks, but he couldn't figure it out. Thing bounded off the bed, crawled up the leg of the chair and worked his way back up to Jeremy's shoulder. Thing lowered his voice an octave, imitating Napoleon. "My name is Napoleon, and I am so strong and handsome."

"Jealous. You're still jealous," Jeremy teased.

He stared at Thing, trying to get him to blink first, but Thing was an expert at this game.

"Excuse me." Devon cleared her throat. "Sorry to interrupt."

Jeremy looked at the computer. Devon was smiling at him.

"Right." Jeremy blushed. "What were we—?"

"Oh," Devon interrupted, sitting up in her chair. "Maybe there's another magic hat here!"

"Another one?" Jeremy said. "How many can there be?"

"Or maybe he's like that crazy lady in Paris."

"Heinke?"

"Yeah, her. Maybe he wants to gain power like she did, take over the world. Oh," Devon grew more excited, "and there's something magical here that will help him do it."

"Aside from the hat he already has? I hope not. But what should we do?" Jeremy asked. "Wait for Travis to get a hold of us?"

"But how can I do anything from up here?" Devon began twirling her hair around her index finger, something Jeremy recognized as a sign that she was thinking or stressed.

"What if I invited you down for Thanksgiving? Do you think your parents would let you come?"

"I'm not sure. Even if they do, that's two weeks away. What if something happens before then?

"Well, Thanksgiving is two weeks away, but maybe you could come down the weekend before. We have the whole week off, don't you?"

"Oh, right," Devon said. "Yes, I do. But still, the Golden Gate Bridge could be the size of a LEGO set by then."

"I know, but I'm not sure we have any other option. Wait," Jeremy added, "you play with LEGOs?"

"No. But I know what they are. Anyways, would your mom want me to come? Aren't you doing something with Sam and his mom? How's it going with you two, anyways?" Jeremy and Sam, the son of his mom's girlfriend, clashed on the Paris trip the previous summer.

"Things are better—" A dirty sock hit Jeremy on the head. He threw it back at Thing. "Sam is actually pretty fun to hang out with. And I'm getting more used to my mom dating." It had taken Jeremy a really long time to get to this point. He'd worried that Sam's mom would steal his own mom away from him.

"I think your mom is more than dating," Devon countered.

"Yeah, I know. Okay. I'm getting more used to it not being just the two of us." Adopted as a baby, Jeremy grew up an only child of a single mom. A single, white mom. Jeremy was Black.

"Well, if you could find a way to get me an invitation, I'll work on my parents." Devon continued to twirl her hair. She'd moved from her bangs to the back of her hair.

"I need a convincing story." Jeremy picked a Rubik's Cube off his desk and twisted it around absentmindedly.

"Tell her I miss Birdbrain," Thing said.

"Aw, how sweet. Thanks, Thing," Birdbrain said.

"Seeing how no one, including Mom, is supposed to know you're magical, I don't think that will work."

"Why don't you just tell your mom you miss Devon?" Thing suggested.

"That's too simple," Jeremy said.

"Maybe not," Devon said. "Tell her you really want to see me, and perhaps add that I don't think we have any plans. I'll do the same here.

2. The Gift

After hanging up with Devon, Jeremy went downstairs.

"Ugh!" Jeremy's mom said just before he entered the room.

Jeremy walked up next to her. "What's up, Mom?"

She looked up from her computer. "I don't have any concrete plans for Thanksgiving week but hoped to take some time off. But work is calling a last minute meeting on the Monday before Thanksgiving. Where is it?" she said, reading through the email. "Well, at least it's here, at the San Francisco office. What? Why are you smiling?"

"I was just talking to Devon. She's feeling really bummed about Thanksgiving 'cause they don't have any plans. Is her dad coming for the meeting? Could I invite Devon if her dad's coming down?"

In the end, Devon and her dad booked flights to come down the Saturday before Thanksgiving. Devon's mom would fly down on Wednesday after work.

The next morning, Jeremy found an envelope with his name on it taped to the top of his skateboard on the front porch. Inside was a postcard of the Grand Lake Theater in Oakland, and scrawled on the back: *TDC* at the top and *Saturday 11/21 at 1 pm* below.

That's the day Devon's coming. Jeremy knew immediately that the note came from Travis, one of two adults in charge of the Travelers Detective Club.

"Mom, what time is Devon arriving on Saturday?"

"Not this Saturday!" she exclaimed.

"No." Jeremy smiled at his mom. "The Saturday before Thanksgiving."

Relief flooded her face. "Whew. I thought I'd missed a week somewhere. Sometime in the morning, I think. Why?"

"I wanted to show her around Grand Avenue and Lakeshore. Maybe catch a movie."

"That's a great idea. The farmer's market is on Saturday, and that's always fun. We can plan to head there after we pick them up from the airport. Perhaps grab some lunch."

"Sounds like a plan." Jeremy paused. "Mom, would it be okay if I went into the city one day this weekend and hung out?"

"What do you mean by hang out? And with whom?"

"I was thinking of asking Sam if he wanted to go."

His mom raised her eyebrows. "Sam? Really? Are you two getting along better?"

"Yeah, a bit." In Paris, he and Sam clashed in part due to Sam's ignorance of the daily racial bias experienced by Jeremy as a Black tween. "I thought we could go over to the Embarcadero and maybe down to Pier 39."

"Let me check in with Cheryl. I don't want you going over there by yourself. Hmm …"

"What?"

"Nothing. Just thinking," his mom said, but there was a twinkle in her eye.

***

Friday night was movie night. Before they settled down with pizza on the couch, Jeremy's mom handed him a wrapped package.

"What's this?" Jeremy turned a small box over in his hands.

"An early Christmas present."

Jeremy tilted his head, eyes narrowing, as he met his mom's gaze. "Why are you giving me an early Christmas present?" Jeremy had no idea what it was.

"You'll see. And I do mean it. This is your main Christmas present. So don't go searching under the tree for much else."

"Okay," Jeremy laughed as he peeled off the wrapping. His jaw dropped. A phone! She'd gotten him a phone! He looked up at his mom, back to the package and at his mom again. "No way! I thought you said I couldn't have one of these until I was in high school."

"If I don't want to have a heart attack while you're off roaming around San Francisco, I need to be able to get a hold of you. And," she touched him on the shoulder to get his full attention, "you need to check in when I ask you to."

"Absolutely. Ye-yes. Su-sure," he stammered, causing his mom to laugh.

Pulling out the cell phone, Jeremy pushed the button to turn it on.

"I think it needs to be charged," his mom said. "And while that's happening, let's go over some ground rules."

Jeremy plugged in the phone charger and sat down on the sofa, biting into a slice of cheese pizza.

"The phone stays here on school days." Jeremy let out a groan. "There's no reason you need it at school, and you're not supposed to have one anyway, per school rules."

"Yeah, but everyone pulls them out over break."

"And you're not everyone."

Jeremy sighed. "Okay."

"And when you're out with your friends, and I ask you to check in at a certain time, I expect you to do so." Jeremy nodded. "And if you don't, the phone goes away, and so does your freedom to roam."

Jeremy nodded again. "Okay. Can we watch the movie now?"

"Um, aren't you forgetting something?"

Jeremy kissed his mom on the cheek, a wide grin on his face. "Thanks, Mom."

***

Cheryl came over with Sam on Saturday morning. Sam, who was white, wore an orange and black San Francisco Giants' t-shirt with matching shoes. While Cheryl and Jeremy's mom drank coffee, the boys went up to Jeremy's room.

"No way. A cell phone? I wish my mom would give me one," Sam said.

"Well, I wouldn't be surprised if you get one soon."

"How ya figure?" Sam asked.

"They're dating, are a couple, or whatever. Your mom will ask mine why she got me a phone, and if you talk about how it's not fair that I have one and you don't, I'm sure she'll cave and get you one too."

"That would be awesome."

Jeremy scrolled through his phone. "Thing!"

"Good morning to you, too," Thing said.

"Hey, Thing," Sam called out. Sam wasn't a part of the Travelers Detective Club, but in Paris, Jeremy and Devon told him about the club, and the magic buddies.

"What were you doing with my phone?" Jeremy interrupted.

"Who, me?"

"Yes, you."

"Whatever gave you the idea I was even near your phone?" Thing backflipped off the top shelf, down to Jeremy's bed where he landed on his tail, bounced up, did a flip and landed on his feet, his hands in the air. "Ta da."

"Show off." Jeremy tilted his head, eyeing Thing curiously. Something was definitely up with Thing. He turned back to his phone, still puzzled. "How about ..." he paused to count, "eighteen selfies of your head up close."

"Oh, that? The camera found me to be so handsome, it kept begging me to take pictures."

Sam laughed. Jeremy shook his head and started for the door.

"Hey, what about me?" Thing called out.

"You sure you want to come? We're taking BART to the city." Jeremy said.

"BART?" Thing asked.

"Bay Area Rapid Transit. You know, the train," Jeremy paused for effect, "that goes through tunnels."

"What?" Thing scoffed. "I'll be fine."

"Okay then." Jeremy said. Thing hopped up onto Jeremy's hand and let himself be attached to the carabiner on Jeremy's backpack.

Scampering down the stairs, Sam laughed and Jeremy smiled as Thing said "Weeeeeee," while sliding down the banister.

"Come back here you two," Jeremy's mom called as they were almost at the front door.

"Yes, Mom?" Jeremy said.

"Let's go over the ground rules again."

"I know them, Mom." Jeremy rolled his eyes and received a glare from his mom. "Sorry."

"What are they, then?" his mom asked.

"We're to call and check in every two hours—"

"Every hour," she corrected.

"Okay, every hour," he said smiling. "Can't blame me for trying."

"And if I text you?"

"I stop what I'm doing and respond right away."

"Thank you. Anything else?" she said, turning to Cheryl.

"No, that's good. Do you guys need money for BART and lunch?"

"Yeah," Jeremy said.

"Sure," Sam said simultaneously.

"What about a jacket?" Jeremy's mom asked, handing him some money.

"Mom, it's beautiful outside. We don't need a jacket."

"You always need to bring something to San Francisco. It could be foggy and cold over there."

Cheryl nodded after handing Sam two ten-dollar bills. "Sam, where's your sweatshirt?"

"Upstairs," he answered sheepishly.

She gave him the cold mom stare that said, 'I told you to bring it with you.'

He ran up to Jeremy's room.

"You too, Jeremy," his mom said.

Jeremy followed Sam upstairs and grabbed his sweatshirt. Racing down the stairs, he stuffed their extra layers into his backpack.

"Well, off you go," Jeremy's mom said. They hurried out the door before their moms could make further demands of them.

Outside the front door, Jeremy stopped. "Wait," he said.

"What?" Sam asked.

"How are we getting to BART?"

"Um." Sam turned and walked back in the house. "Um, Mom," he called out sheepishly again, "can we have a ride to BART?"

His mom came around the corner, keys in hand. "I wondered when you'd figure that out."

3. A Trip to S.F.

Cheryl dropped them off at the curb in front of the station. The boys thanked her for the ride. At the gate, they put their Clipper Cards on the turnstile, walked through and headed to the escalator.

"You sounded pretty intent on getting into San Francisco today. Any particular reason?" Sam asked.

Jeremy recounted what he'd heard on the news as they rode up the escalator. "And then Mom had a work meeting scheduled at the last minute which means Devon can come since her dad works for Tech too. Remember when Travis admitted that Tech sends our parents where they need Devon and I or other detectives to go?"

"Yeah," Sam said. In Paris, Sam helped Jeremy, Devon and Addie after art work and important landmarks, including the Eiffel Tower, disappeared.

"So, what's your plan?" Sam asked, as they stepped off the escalator.

"I don't really have one."

"He's consistent that way," Thing said.

"You know I brought my backpack for a reason," Jeremy threatened.

"Fffftt."

"What was that?" Sam asked.

"That was me, sticking my tongue out at Jeremy if I had a tongue—"

"Yeah, yeah. Thing, that gets old," Jeremy said.

"...or a mouth," Thing finished. "Well, I've never told him. And please don't tell me you're going to be grouchy today."

An announcement came overhead: "San Francisco train now approaching Platform One."

Jeremy shook his head and stepped onto the train after other passengers disembarked.

"Why are you always shaking your head?" Thing asked.

"Because of you. Now shush."

"Don't sh—" Thing started, but Jeremy stopped him with a glare, silently reminding him that he was supposed to be quiet and not draw attention to himself. Thing struggled with this rule every time he left the house.

After they sat down, Jeremy adjusted his backpack to ensure Thing could look out the window. "I don't really have a plan but thought we'd go to the Embarcadero and maybe walk down to Pier 39. It's touristy like Union Square, and it could be the next target."

Sam observed Thing while Jeremy talked. He turned back to Jeremy. "I wish I could have one of those."

"One of what? Oh, Thing? I'm not sure how that would happen. He just came in a box to my doorstep one day. I'm not sure who picked me or why, to be honest." Jeremy watched the view as they came out of the tunnel under downtown Oakland and approached the West Oakland station. "Okay, remember, Thing. We have another, longer tunnel coming up, but we'll get off at the first stop."

In answer to Sam's questioning gaze, Jeremy whispered, "He's afraid of tunnels."

"I'm not ... why do you have to go telling everyone?" Thing complained. "If you keep doing that I'm gonna tell on you."

"What's there to tell?" Jeremy asked.

"I'm not telling," Thing said. Entering the Transbay Tube, it became darker, and the noise, a loud, continuous, high-pitched squeal, made it difficult to carry on a conversation.

Several minutes later the train slowed to a stop, the doors opened, and Jeremy and Sam walked onto the station platform. "You can open your eyes now, Thing," Jeremy said. Two escalators later, they emerged onto the streets of San Francisco, facing the Ferry Building and the San Francisco Bay.

High-rise buildings lined the street, as did homeless people down on their luck. The clear sky held a cool breeze. Over his shoulder Jeremy could see a thin layer of fog rolling into the city. After crossing the Embarcadero, they stopped to listen to the drum guy. Headphones on, sweat glistening and sticks blazing, the man beat out a rhythm on an array of homemade drums. Twenty plus buckets and metal cans, all dented, rang with complicated rhythms, accompanying music only he could hear.

"I love this guy!" Sam started dancing, clearly not caring that he looked ridiculous.

Jeremy doubled over laughing. Sam pushed Jeremy playfully causing Jeremy to backpedal to keep his balance. Both smiling, they continued across the street. "He's out here almost every time Mom and I come to the city," Jeremy said.

After buying snacks at a bakery in the Ferry Building, the boys walked out back along the ferry dock, dodging passengers disembarking from the recent arrival. "You game to head down to Pier 39?" Jeremy asked.

"Yeah. Oops, I meant to stop on the way here. Can we backtrack first?"

"Sure, what do you need?" Jeremy asked.

"I wanted to stop by the Giants' Dugout store."

"What's that?"

"What's that?" Sam asked, incredulously. "Oh right, you don't follow the Giants at all, do you?"

"Nope. Baseball is too boring."

Sam shook his head. They headed to the store where Sam wandered around, looking at the merchandise. He eventually settled on a pocket schedule for the upcoming season. Jeremy walked around aimlessly, bored.

"That it?" Jeremy asked.

"Yeah. It's just fun to look. I don't have enough money to buy anything, yet. I'm saving up for a new jersey."

"Can we head down to Fisherman's Wharf now?" Jeremy had enough of baseball for the year.

"Sure. Hey, have you noticed anything different with our moms since we got back from Paris?"

"Like what?"

"I don't know. I thought I saw Mom searching real estate websites. I was just wondering if you'd noticed anything."

"Nope." Jeremy stopped midstep. "Wait. What are you saying?"

Sam shrugged his shoulders. "I'm wondering if they're thinking of moving in together."

Jeremy didn't want to hear it. "Or maybe your mom just wants to move." Jeremy didn't wait for a response but started walking again.

Sam caught up to him a moment later. They walked in silence, the bay waters visible between buildings on their right. Sam risked a "Thanks," when Jeremy stopped to pull out their sweatshirts. The fog moved in during their short time inside. It blanketed the city, making it a good twenty degrees cooler than in Oakland when they left.

As they neared Fisherman's Wharf, the boys meandered around and through groups of tourists pausing to consult maps or eyeing some attraction; they tended to take up a majority of the sidewalk. Some of the tourists wore brand new sweatshirts with San Francisco logos and scenes on them. The fact that they were also wearing shorts meant they were unaware and unprepared for how quickly a sunny day could turn foggy and cold.

"Hey, wasn't there supposed to be a Christmas tree down here?" Sam stopped and pointed toward the end of the boardwalk.

"Was there?" Jeremy said, alarmed. "I actually don't come here that often."

"You did say one tree disappeared, right?"

Jeremy nodded.

"Let's find out if there was one here, too." They wandered over to the ticket kiosk for Alcatraz tours at Pier 33 and approached a ticket agent.

"Excuse me," Sam said. "Isn't there usually a Christmas tree further down by Pier 39, or is it still too early?"

"I'm not sure. I thought they started to put one up, but when I got to work today it was gone. Probably some city regulation."

"Thanks," Sam said.

They continued on the promenade in the direction of Pier 39. A man dressed entirely in silver from his hair to his shoes stood as still as a statue, imitating a tourist peering through binoculars. Another man, colored in gold, stood with his hand at his forehead, blocking a non-existent sun from obscuring his vision. He peered out at a crowd of tourists standing around waiting to see if he would blink.

"So now the guy collects Christmas trees?" Sam wondered aloud.

"I know. Doesn't make sense. Why come all the way here to steal Christmas trees? Unless ..." Jeremy stopped talking as they turned and wandered to look at the sea lions perched on a dock at Pier 39.

"Unless what?"

"Unless he's just getting started. Actually, I'm sure he's just getting started. In Paris he started small, well smallish. He stole really famous art, but size wise they were small."

"Yeah, then he moved on to famous landmarks," Sam said.

"But why now?" Jeremy paused. Several of the twenty or so sea lions piled on the pier started barking at one another. Sam and Jeremy stopped to watch. "Is he just trying to cause chaos over the holidays or—wait just a second. My phone. Oh crap, what time is it?"

"Um, later than we want it to be," Sam said, as Jeremy answered the phone.

"Hi Mom … yeah I know, sorry. Lost track of time … I know … At Pier 39, just got here." Jeremy turned away from the sea lions and headed back toward the main promenade. "Okay, yes.… Can I have one more shot?... Okay, thanks, Mom." Jeremy pushed the red button on his phone to end the call. "Let me set my alarm, so I remember to text her."

"Hey, I thought Thing was orange," Sam said.

"Yeah, he is."

"Well, he isn't now."

Jeremy shrugged off his backpack because he couldn't see Thing with it on. Thing was yellow. "We have to go back."

"What?"

"We have to go back. When Thing turns yellow, it means we missed a clue somewhere."

The boys retraced their footsteps. Just before they reached the entrance to Pier 39, Thing turned blue. "Stop. Look around for anything that could be a clue," Jeremy said.

"Can't Thing just tell us?" Sam asked.

"No. He doesn't know what we're looking for, his body just changes colors. Blue means there's something here."

They combed the ground in the surrounding area. Trash littered the pier. Empty beverage containers and pamphlets for various tours and activities were strewn about. The boys gave up their search after several groups of people bumped into them.

As Jeremy stepped aside, his gaze wandered to the man in silver now holding the pose of the Statue of Liberty. Jeremy started walking toward him, glancing at Thing as he went. When Jeremy stood directly in front of the silver man, Thing turned bright blue. Jeremy noticed a brown pamphlet in the man's left hand, different from the other papers lying around. Jeremy tried to grab it, but the man's hand tightened around the paper, his eyes widening.

"Sam, do you have any money left?"

"Yeah."

"Can I have it?"

"Um, okay." Sam pulled out a five dollar bill. Jeremy took it, showed it to the street artist, who allowed him to remove the pamphlet and replaced it with the money. Thing returned to his normal orange self.

The pamphlet advertised the Golden Gate Model Railroad Museum in Point Richmond. "Ever been there?" Jeremy asked Sam.

"No. You?"

"No. Don't even know where it is. Near Richmond, I guess," Jeremy said. "Hey," he continued, "it says here that they run the trains at the museum on Sundays. What if we try and get our moms to take us tomorrow? Check it out?"

"Sure. But isn't that for little kids?"

"Don't know. But my mom is always saying that she wishes I would stop growing up, so I'll play that angle to get her to take us."

4. The Train Museum

Jeremy and Sam were able to convince their moms to take them to the museum the next day, though they didn't leave until well after lunch. Twenty minutes later, they exited the freeway and drove through Point Richmond, a small town Jeremy had never heard of. A short tunnel—Thing closed his eyes—emptied them onto the edge of a tree-studded park with green grass that abutted a beach. A quarter mile later, a sign for the museum appeared on the left.

As they were pulling in, Sam jabbed Jeremy in the side. "Look," he whispered.

Jeremy caught a glimpse of the driver pulling out of the parking lot. A white, clean-shaven man with a dark green newsboy cap on his head sat at the wheel. His dark brown hair hung below his ears. Jeremy remembered coming face to face with this same man in Portugal and Paris. "That's him!" Jeremy whispered. He turned his head to follow the car until it was out of sight.

"Does he wear that hat all the time?" Sam wondered.

"Well, at least we know we're on the right track," Jeremy said.

"Ha. That's funny," Thing said after they were out of the car and walking behind their moms.

"What's funny?" Jeremy asked.

"You said we're on the right track, and we're going to see trains … on tracks. Get it?"

"Yeah, yeah."

After buying tickets for Jeremy and Sam, their moms left them on their own and went across the street to go for a walk in the park. The boys headed up a set of stairs and through an open door.

"Dang," Sam remarked.

"Yeah, dang is right. This is not what I expected."

They entered a building the size of a large warehouse. On the left lay a setup of a small city, complete with a river, and motorized trolley. Not only were there multiple miniature buildings but also cars and fire trucks, stop lights and people.

A mountain rose behind and extended to the opposite end of the warehouse, running three different trains over multiple railroad tracks. Two men were standing at a control platform, monitoring the trains. On the other side of the narrow walkway were several more train tracks.

As he examined the models, Jeremy realized they were recreations of various train stations throughout the Bay Area, complete with replicas of the surrounding terrain. Different sized trains and tracks were utilized and after reading the pamphlet, Jeremy learned there were three main layouts of train tracks with as many different sizes of trains. The detail to which the hobbyists went to recreate the scenery amazed him.

After spending time examining the various trains, Jeremy approached a man standing behind a plastic partition separating the trains and hobbyists from visitors. "Excuse me. Did you see a man about yay high," Jeremy held his hand slightly over his head, "wearing a hat that was kind of flat with a …" Jeremy searched for the word, "... with a …" He couldn't think of the word and moved his hand back and forth in front of his head.

"A brim?"

Jeremy nodded.

"Yes, as a matter of fact I did. Why?"

"Just curious. Did he ask any questions?"

"Funny you should ask."

"Why?"

"'Cause he didn't ask questions. He just boasted about his own setup."

"What kind of setup?"

"He said he was making one of San Francisco but instead of trains it would have cable cars, Coit Tower and the Ferry Building, some Christmas trees and even the Golden Gate Bridge."

"Anything else?"

"Maybe … I can't remember."

"Okay, thanks." Jeremy and Sam walked away.

They walked to the end of the warehouse where a N scale train ran a circuitous route above them. "What do we do now?" Sam asked.

Jeremy shook his head. "Too bad we didn't get his license plate. We could have tried to track—what, Thing?"

Thing was kicking Jeremy's leg from the carabiner clip. "I got it."

"Got what?" Jeremy asked.

"The license plate."

"You … wait. What? You got the license plate?"

Thing's eyes brightened. "Yes … I … did."

"How'd ya do that?"

"Paid attention. Unlike someone I know," Thing snickered.

"Guys," Sam interjected. "What good will that do? I mean, good job Thing, but what are we going to do with that information? I don't think you can just Google a license plate."

"You're probably right." Jeremy sighed. "I was just hoping for some kind of clue, something to point us in the right direction.… Any direction, actually."

"Well, we know he drives a blue … a Toyota of some kind. And

Thing knows the license plate. That information could be useful later. Let's make sure to write it down so we don't forget," Sam added.

***

Jeremy emailed Devon later that night, filling her in on the weekend's events. Moments later a Zoom invite arrived in his in-box. He clicked on it.

"Hey, what's up?" he asked.

Devon was twisting her hair around her index finger. Without preamble she launched into their conversation. "So this man traveled all the way to Portugal, then Paris and now San Francisco because he wants to build his own model railroad set? He tried stealing landmarks in Paris and now he's stealing Christmas trees in San Francisco for decoration? That doesn't make sense."

"When you put it that way, no, it doesn't," Jeremy said. "But why then? That far-right crazy lady, Heinke. wanted to take over the world. But we never figured out this guy's goal. He's the one who stole the medallions and stones out of the statue in Portugal, not her."

"You're right," she said. "Remember when we met with Travis after dinner in Paris? He said those responsible for releasing the crushed man from St. Thomas Aquinas' reliquary were right-wing extremists who opposed immigration and people of color in power. They wanted Paris and the European Union to descend into chaos."

"Yeah, and Travis thought Heinke might be involved," Jeremy said.

"That's right. And while she turned out to be an extremist, she didn't have anything to do with the reliquary disappearance. The guy with the hat did. Hat Man."

"Oh, is that what we're calling him?"

"Yep." Devon said.

"While our parent's company tracked Heinke's group," Jeremy said, "Travis focused on Hat Man. Did Travis think they were all part of the same organization? He didn't seem to know who this Hat Man was when he showed up in Portugal. I'm confused."

"Me too."

"Wow, you guys sure are confused a lot," Thing called over from the bed where he lounged on Jeremy's pillow.

"Hey, Thing," Devon called out.

"Hi. Tell Birdbrain I said hi."

"I will."

Jeremy ignored the interruption. "Was Travis right that this guy is out to destabilize governments? Or was his intel wrong? Maybe this guy just wants the world's best model train display."

"There are crazy adults in this world—" Devon said.

"You can say that again," Thing commented.

"—but that would be extra crazy," Devon finished.

Jeremy and Devon went back and forth trying to figure out the how and why of it all in addition to coordinating for the weekend. Jeremy wanted to do more exploring in San Francisco before Devon arrived, but because of school, he'd have to wait.

5. Devon Comes to Town

Over the next week there were almost nightly reports of mysterious happenings in San Francisco. The life-sized, two-story gingerbread house at the Fairmont Hotel disappeared. "This San Francisco tradition," said Teresa Estasio of Channel 4 News, "involving eight thousand gingerbread bricks and five months of preparation has disappeared into thin air. As you can see there is nothing left, not even a crumb."

Later in the week, two cable cars went missing. When reporters interviewed people on the streets, passersby said things like, "... makes me nervous," and "What's next?" While Jeremy didn't understand the stock market, he recognized the stress on traders' faces when the news reported on the several hundred point drop over the last three days of the week. There were calls for the mayor to find the beloved cable cars or resign.

Jeremy felt frustrated and helpless. He had to go to school, and he needed Devon's help but had to wait until Saturday for her to arrive. With each disappearance his irritation grew exponentially. His mom, worried about his stress level, forbade him from watching the news Thursday night. She forgot he could get the information he wanted on his phone and computer.

***

Saturday morning, Jeremy and his mom picked up Devon and her dad at the airport. After dropping off luggage at their hotel, the four of them went down to Lake Merritt to meet Sam and Cheryl for lunch at the farmer's market. The market, set up across from the lake, consisted of multiple white tents lined up between Grand and Lakeshore Avenues. Separated from the farmer's stalls by a short walkway were more tents selling hot food, from tamales to Indian curry to crepes to dumplings. A truck selling rotisserie chicken and potatoes parked on the street. Smells of garlic, onions, curry, barbeque, and others he couldn't identify, bombarded Jeremy, making him all the more hungry. Everyone grabbed their desired lunch and went to sit on a grassy knoll behind the food stalls.

After promising to stay together, Jeremy, Devon and Sam were given permission to go off on their own, provided they checked in hourly. They crossed the street to check out the movies at the Grand Lake Theater. They were too early to meet Travis, the head of human resources for Jeremy's mom's and Devon's dad's company but also second in command of the TDC. Jeremy knew he sent the card setting up the meeting at one o'clock.

Devon, Jeremy and Sam wandered over to Arizmendi, a bakery co-op, to grab some pastries; Devon a scone, Sam a chocolate cookie and Jeremy a brioche filled with chunks of chocolate.

Retracing their steps with pastries in hand, they spotted Travis under the theater's marquee. A Black man over six feet tall and sporting a shaved head, Travis indicated that they should follow him. He walked ahead down Grand Avenue. Outside Walden Pond Books, Travis stopped and waited for them to catch up.

"Good afternoon. I thought we should meet away from the farmer's market in case your parents were still around," he said.

All three of them greeted him. Travis continued. "I'm assuming you've heard about the disappearances?"

They nodded. "The two Christmas trees, the gingerbread house at the Fairmont Hotel and at least two cable cars, right?" Jeremy said. "We think we know what else he's after." Jeremy told him about his and Sam's trip to San Francisco and the model train museum. "Does he have any connection to Heinke, that woman in Paris? Does he want some new world order? It seems silly to just do it so he can have his own model train display."

Travis stood quietly for a moment, shifting a small box from his left to his right hand. "We think he might be trying to cause instability in the global markets. The global financial markets," he added. "If people panic, there is potential for big swings in the stock market that if timed correctly, could make someone very, very rich. We saw that happen briefly in Europe after the Sacré-Cœur and Eiffel Tower disappeared. There's also the possibility that he likes the feeling of control he gains by causing panic."

"Back in Paris," Devon said, "when you mentioned those who were responsible for removing the stones and medallion from the statue in Portugal and using them to bring the crushed man under the column at the reliquary to life, you said they were members of a hate group." Devon absentmindedly twirled her hair with her finger. "Are you saying they aren't trying to take over governments anymore? That they're just after money?"

"I'm not sure," Travis replied. "I mistakenly thought that Heinke's group revived the crushed man. They certainly could be after both money and power."

The group fell silent for a moment.

"Is Addie coming to help us?" Devon asked. Devon and Sam met Addie over the summer in Paris when they foiled attempts to steal works of art from the Louvre and the Musee D'orsay, along with the Sacré-Cœur and the Eiffel Tower. That same thief left the train museum as the boys arrived the previous Sunday. At that time he wore the magic hat that allowed him to shrink the Eiffel Tower into a four-inch miniature figurine.

"No, she isn't. Thanksgiving is an American holiday, not a French one, and she doesn't have this week off from school. Her dad's here for our meeting, but she stayed behind with her mom." Travis paused. "Which brings me to this." He held up the box in his right hand. "We feel that you will need as much help as you can get, and not having Addie here was an unexpected setback. This has never been allowed before, but Baako, the original magic buddy, must have felt it important and allowable because she created this." Travis handed the box to Sam.

Sam's eyes grew wide. "What?"

"Open it," Travis instructed. The side of his mouth twitched.

Sam tore open the box and pulled out a hand-sized, stuffed Basset Hound with a TDC patch on the back and a carabiner clip. Sam's mouth dropped open. Devon broke into a grin, and Jeremy said, "Nice."

"Does this mean …?" Sam's voice tapered off as if he was scared to ask his question.

"Welcome to the Travelers Detective Club, Sam." Travis gave him a big smile.

6. The New Buddy

Sam stood with his new magic buddy in his hand, momentarily frozen. "How do I turn it on?"

"They'll show you," Travis said. "But not just yet. I need all of you to know that we're short on time. The disappearance of the Eiffel Tower over the summer caused unease over not just France but the entire world. Now that it's starting again, if he moves on to bigger things than Christmas trees and cable cars, it won't take long before people panic."

"Ahem." Jeremy looked down at his side. Thing stared at Travis, eyes narrowed. Thing didn't like it when someone used his name in a sentence.

"Sorry, Thing," Travis said, smiling.

"Still sensitive, I see," Devon said.

"Oh, Travis."

"Yes, Jeremy."

"I almost forgot. We got the license—" Jeremy paused, because Thing kicked him in the side.

"Sorry. Thing got the license plate number off the car at the train museum. Is there a way you can use it to find out who the man is, or where he lives?"

Travis's eyes widened. "We should be able to. This is great news."

After taking the license plate number along with Jeremy's cell phone information, Travis left the three members of the TDC to be on their own.

"How do I turn this on?" Sam asked, looking down at the dog.

"You squeeze it," Jeremy said.

With his face lit with anticipation, Sam squeezed the dog.

Nothing happened.

Sam squeezed again, doing so for a full ten seconds.

Nothing happened.

Sam's face became crestfallen.

"Ha! Just kidding," came a deep, resonating voice from the dog.

"What!" Sam said. "Oh, I guess all these buddies try to have a sense of humor."

"Try?" Thing said incredulously.

"I think we're rather successful," added Birdbrain.

"Who are you?" the dog asked Sam.

"Sam."

"Do you have a name for me, Sam? Only remember, German Shepherds such as myself demand a strong name."

"German Shepherd?" Sam said. "You're not a German Shepherd. You're more like a Basset Hound."

"Excuse me, I am not. Wait, am I?" he asked, his voice changing from deep and commanding to small, almost whimpering, and full of self doubt.

"Ok, wow. I have a magic buddy with a personality conflict. What's a good name for him?" Sam asked. "Or should I pick two?"

"Ha, ha, very funny," the dog said.

"Hey, while you're deciding," Jeremy said, "can we get some more food? There's a place back on Lakeshore that has good hot dogs."

"Sure," Sam and Devon echoed.

Walking into Top Dog, Sam started chuckling.

"How's H.D. for a name?" he said to no one in particular.

"As long as it stands for Handsome Dude, it sounds good to me," said the dog.

"Well, I was thinking more of Hot Dog but you can believe what you'd like," Sam said with a smile.

"That's original," said Jeremy, chuckling.

"Says the guy who named his buddy Thing," countered Devon.

Laughing, the boys grabbed their hot dogs—Devon declined yet more food— and sat down at a corner booth. The place smelled like hot dogs, ketchup and root beer. Spilled sodas stuck to the table, thus the root beer smell. The Beatles' "Yellow Submarine" played in the background.

"Hey," Thing whispered to Jeremy, "are you going to let me say hi to Birdbrain and this guy?" He pointed to H.D.

Jeremy looked around. They were the only ones in the shop besides the employee behind the counter, preoccupied with his phone. Jeremy met Devon's eyes. She nodded. "But let's put them down on the seat, just in case," she added.

While the buddies hung out, Devon reviewed what they knew so far. "So the man we are after got the stones and medallions in Portugal from the statue of King John after we left, he used them to free the crushed man under the column at St. Aquinas's reliquary and used the hat to shrink and attempt to steal several monuments and pieces of art …"

"… before we stopped him," Sam interrupted.

"Right," Devon continued. "Only, he got away with the hat, and now he's stealing Christmas trees, giant gingerbread houses, cable cars and important San Francisco landmarks in order to cause financial panic, upset governments—"

"Or to set up the world's best miniature train set," Sam finished.

"And we have his license plate number which Travis may be able to put to good use," Jeremy added. "That's about all we have, right?"

"Well, and the fact that I'm now an official member of the TDC, and H.D. here, mister Basset Hound aka German Shepherd, might be able to help. I wonder what his magic powers are?" Sam added.

"Well, ours only changed colors their first year," Devon said. "They got new powers before the second trip."

"Yeah, Thing could throw up invisible walls that people ran right into ..." Jeremy said.

"... and Birdbrain could actually fly," Devon added.

"Well, I hope I don't have to wait too long for H.D. to show his powers. Otherwise, how helpful could he be?" Sam said.

"I heard that," came a deep voice from the bench seat.

***

"We can't just wander around San Francisco, hoping we bump into him," Devon said. "We need to find a way to get ahead of him."

Jeremy's phone pinged.

"Travis sent me the address associated with the license plate. It's an Oakland address."

Jeremy, Devon and Sam were hanging out on a grassy hill along Lake Merritt. Their parents went for a walk around the lake.

"Is it close?" Sam asked.

"Let me check." Jeremy punched the address into his Maps app. "It's not too far, but not walking distance. About two miles away. It's over near the Oakland/Berkeley border."

Sam stood up and looked around.

"What?" Jeremy asked.

Sam pointed toward the Grand Lake Theater. "What about using one of those scooters?"

"That's a great idea," Jeremy said. "Let's go."

Jeremy got up, but Devon stopped him. "Wait," she said. "We get to that address, and then what?"

Jeremy eyed her before slowly sitting back down.

"We need a plan," Devon added.

"We could snoop around the house, and see if the hat is there," Sam said.

"Said the white boy who doesn't seem to worry about getting the police called on him," Jeremy said incredulously. "You realize we are sitting near where a white woman called the police on Black people barbequing. You do know about Barbeque Becky, right? And you want me to go snooping around someone's house? No, thank you. You let me know how that goes."

"Okay, okay…. Bad idea," Sam said apologetically.

"Ludicrous," Birdbrain chirped.

"Huh?" Sam said.

"Ignore her," Devon said.

Jeremy shook his head, as he stared momentarily at the ground.

"What if there was a way to track the car?" Sam asked.

Jeremy lifted his head and smiled. "There is."

"GPS," Devon added. "And it just happens that—"

"—our parents work in the technology industry." Jeremy met Devon's gaze.

"What? You just happen to have a GPS tracking device lying around?" Sam asked.

"No," Jeremy pulled out his phone and started texting. "But Travis might."

"Can I see your phone, Jeremy?" Devon asked.

"Sure." Jeremy finished and handed her the phone.

"What's your address?"

Jeremy told her, and she entered it into the phone. "He's only about a mile from your house."

7. Thing's New Power

Early the next morning Jeremy went out to his front porch and found the small box Travis left for him. Inside was a magnetic tracking device and instructions on how to sync it to his phone. He ran upstairs, grabbed a jacket and started out the door.

"Hey! What about me?"

"Oh, right. Sorry," Jeremy apologized to Thing. "Though I'm not sure you can help me."

"Whatcha doing?"

"Gonna try and place a GPS tracker on a car."

"What happened to not snooping around other people's houses as a Black kid?" Thing asked.

Jeremy stopped midstride. "Right…. Guess I'm being pretty stupid."

"I think I can help you," Thing said casually while doing a

backflip on Jeremy's desk.

"How?"

"First you need to apologize for suggesting that I couldn't."

"Are we really doing this?"

Thing glared at Jeremy.

"Okay…. I'm sorry I assumed you couldn't help me. Wait…."
Jeremy spun around, trying to find Thing. "Where are you?" As his
eyes came back around to his starting point, Jeremy found Thing
back on the desk. "Where'd you go?"

"Nowhere." Thing's eyes sparkled, and Jeremy knew Thing
would have a gigantic grin on his face if he had a mouth.

"What do you mean nowhere? You disap— see you just did it
again."

Thing reappeared in exactly the same spot.

"Wait a second…." Jeremy's body tingled, his excitement
building. "Do you have a new magical power?"

"Hold out your hand," Thing requested. After he jumped into
Jeremy's outstretched hand, he directed Jeremy to stand in front of
his mirror. "Okay, so I'm not sure if this will work, but I have a
feeling…. Now you see us … and now you don't."

Jeremy let out a whoop and started dancing in front of the mirror
which provided no reflection. He and Thing were invisible. "This is
crazy!"

"What's crazy is your dancing," Thing said. "Who taught you to dance? I've never seen a Black person dance like that."

"What do you mean? When have you seen Black people dance?"

"YouTube. And it's definitely obvious you were raised by a white woman."

"Will you stop? Look at us! Just look at us!"

"Can't. We're invisible. Ha!" Thing exclaimed while doing a backflip on Jeremy's hand. While Thing was in midair, Jeremy's reflection flashed in the mirror.

"Wait, what just happened?" Jeremy asked.

"It seems that you have to be holding me for this to work," Thing said. "Most unfortunate."

"But still, this is awesome!" Jeremy grinned at Thing. "How did you figure that one out?"

"It just happened. Same as when I realized I could put up invisible walls. Last summer, the morning we went to Paris, and I woke you up by jumping on your face, you threw a sock at me, remember?"

"Yeah, and you told me it was a good thing I didn't play baseball 'cause I missed."

"Well, that's still true. You shouldn't play baseball. But for once your aim was good. The sock stopped in midair. I put up a wall automatically, as if I knew I could. And yesterday I was ... well, never mind what I was doing, but I was in front of the mirror and made myself disappear."

Jeremy smiled. "What were you doing in front of the mirror?"

Thing ignored the question. "The point is, I can help you put the tracking device on the car."

Jeremy stood still, looking at his reflection which he could again see in the mirror. "I just realized I can't take a scooter 'cause I don't have a credit card. Let me see how far away it is … oh, right, Devon said about a mile." Jeremy checked the map on his phone. "Yep, she was right. We can walk it. Okay, let's go." Jeremy hooked Thing's carabiner to a belt loop of his jeans and headed downstairs.

"Morning," his mom called out.

Jeremy froze. "Um ... Hi, Mom."

"What are you up to?" she asked suspiciously.

"Nothing."

His mom's left eyebrow disappeared, rising high enough to be obscured by her hair. "Try again," she insisted.

Jeremy paused, his mind whirling. "I wanted to go over to the skateboard park."

"This early?"

Jeremy shrugged. "I got up early, and I'm bored."

"Bring your phone. And Jeremy."

"Yes, Mom?"

"Mind yourself and be careful."

"You know I will be."

"Back by ten, but text me in one hour. And grab something to eat, please."

"Thanks, Mom." Jeremy gave her a kiss on the cheek, took a banana and granola bar from the kitchen and raced out the door.

Grabbing his skateboard off the front porch, Jeremy started up the street, walking at first due to the incline. He ate while he walked. Once out of sight of his house, Jeremy pulled out his phone and found a route to the address Travis texted him. Alternately walking and riding his skateboard, he arrived in under fifteen minutes. He double checked the license plate of the blue car in the driveway with the one Thing had given him. "That's it," Jeremy said.

He rode his skateboard back around the corner, glanced over his shoulder, and ditched it behind some bushes.

"Okay, Thing. Can you make us invisible now?"

"You have to hold me."

Jeremy grabbed Thing.

"Ouch!"

"Oops sor—"

"Just kidding."

"Always the jokester." Jeremy looked down. He could no longer see himself. "This is so crazy. Cool, but crazy."

"Let's get going. I don't know if there's a time limit on how long I can keep this up."

"Time ... what? Now you tell me?" Jeremy ignored the worried whispers that were telling him to stop. He hurried off back around the corner and up to the car. Even though he was invisible, the whispers turned into loud rumblings that he would get caught. His hands were shaking as he took the magnetic GPS sensor out of his pocket. Only then did the stupidity of his plan hit him. Was that a door opening? He couldn't breathe. The tracker slipped out of his sweaty grip. Having to work one handed made it more difficult and stressful. Jeremy picked up the tracker and placed it under the bumper of the car. He sprinted back to his skateboard. Once Jeremy ensured the streets were still empty, he let go of Thing.

"Wow, your hands are wet," Thing said.

Jeremy took some deep, steadying breaths. "Yeah," he finally managed. He headed down the sidewalk on his skateboard, trying to dodge the cracks in the cement made by trees pushing through the concrete. Two blocks later he stopped again.

"What?" Thing asked.

"That didn't take as long as I thought. Should probably go to the skateboard park for a bit before heading home. Just need to think how to get there from here. I'm pretty sure we're close. Oh, right. I can use my phone." Jeremy pulled out his phone, checked his location and confirmed his route. Back on his board again, he skated down the middle of the quiet street to avoid the uneven sidewalk. He wasn't worried about traffic; he hadn't seen a car drive by since he first ditched his board in the bushes.

A car approached slowly from behind, so Jeremy steered his

board toward the side of the road, but nothing passed. The low rumble of the car engine stayed with him. Unnerved, Jeremy turned to look over his shoulder and almost crashed. He stumbled off his board and came to a stop.

8. The Encounter

"Where are you headed?" A white police officer leaned out of his open patrol car window.

With difficulty Jeremy caught his breath, trying not to panic. His pulse pounded in his ears. He knew about this of course; his mom had had the talk with him. But still, it was his first time. What had she told him? He couldn't remember.

"Um, the skateboard park," Jeremy said.

"What was that you put in your pocket?" the officer asked.

"What? This?" Jeremy started to reach for his pocket, when the officer yelled at him.

"Keep your hands where I can see them!"

Jeremy held his arms out from his side. Confusion and fear flooded his senses. He stood frozen, as the officer got out of his car parked in the middle of the road.

"It's just a cell phone, sir." Jeremy said as the officer approached.

"Where did you get it?"

"My mom."

"Right." The officer spoke, his tone filled with doubt.

Jeremy suddenly felt chilled.

"I can—hey!" Jeremy didn't finish his sentence because the officer pulled the phone out of his pocket. "That's mine!"

"We'll see about that." The officer pushed the button on the bottom to engage the screen.

"You can't do that … just take my phone and—" He looked up. The officer's eyes bore into Jeremy's.

"We can take this downtown if you'd like," the officer said.

Something his mom told him came back, sharp, into his consciousness. *Your job is to get home safely. I can ask questions later. That's my job. You just get home.*

Jeremy kept his mouth shut.

The officer searched through his phone. Jeremy stared at the ground, fighting hard not to say something. The officer held the phone out to Jeremy, showing a picture of him and his mom. "Who's that?"

"My mom." The words came out half croak, half whisper. Jeremy's mouth was dry, his throat constricted.

After a pause, the officer handed back the phone. "Guess it's yours."

To Jeremy, he seemed almost disappointed. Jeremy remained frozen, his feet like cement fixed to the pavement.

"Be on your way," the officer commanded.

A deep sadness made Jeremy want to hang his head and cry all the way home, but a part of him wanted to race back as quickly as possible. He climbed on his skateboard and let it roll him slowly home.

Jeremy dropped his skateboard on the porch and walked into the door.

"Your back ear—" From the couch, Jeremy's mom glanced up from her book. "What's wrong, Jeremy?"

Jeremy stood just inside the front door. A shiver drove through his body, like when you get out of the pool with a cool wind blowing. The shiver grew to a tremble. Eyes glistening, tears rolled down his cheeks.

His mom reached him in two steps and enveloped him in a hug. Shaking, he cried on his mother's shoulder for several moments. When his tears dried up, and his body stilled, his mother led him over to the couch. She was a quiet, reassuring presence as his story spilled out, his eyes staring at nothing in particular on the wood floor. When he finished, he looked up into his mom's glistening eyes. She hugged him again, and they sat in silence for some time.

"You did good, Jeremy. You made it home."

"But it's not fair. It's not right." Jeremy settled deeper into his mom's arms.

"I know. You are absolutely right." His mom ran her fingers over his hair, something that always calmed him. "It's not fair…. Jeremy, where were you when this happened?"

"A few blocks from the skateboard park."

"Any chance you got his badge number?

"No, why?"

"Because I'm going to call and lodge a complaint."

Jeremy sat up and faced his mom. "No ... Mom ... don't."

His fear must have been visible because she reached out and pulled him close again. "I have to sweetie, I have to." They remained on the couch, not speaking, Jeremy resting in his mother's arms.

***

"Watch this everyone," Thing said. Devon and Sam walked into Jeremy's room together, having arrived moments earlier. Thing had clearly been waiting for this moment. "Now you see me … now you don't."

"Wow," Devon said.

"That's so cool," Sam said.

"Yeah, and if Jeremy holds me I can make him invisible," Thing added.

"That's incredible," Devon said.

"No way!" Sam said. "You must be psyched," he said to Jeremy.

Jeremy shrugged, his enthusiasm dampened by his experience earlier in the morning.

"What? You're not excited about that?" Sam said.

Someone knocked on Jeremy's door.

"Yeah?" Jeremy called out.

A man's head peaked out from around the door.

"Hey, Michael," Jeremy said. "Whatcha doin here?"

Michael was a family friend, becoming a kind of big brother to Jeremy over the years.

"Your mom called and told me what happened this morning and asked me to come by."

"What happened this morning?" Sam asked.

Not answering him, Jeremy got up off his bed. "Guys, can you give me a minute? I'll be back in a few."

Jeremy walked out of the room without a backwards glance and followed Michael down the stairs and out onto the front porch. They both sat down on the steps.

"How are you?" Michael asked.

Jeremy shrugged. "I don't know. Feeling like I want to hide in my house and not come out for a long time." His feelings of anger and shame boiled up to the surface. "Why'd he have to do that? I wasn't doing anything, just riding my board." Jeremy paused. That wasn't exactly true, though he definitely wasn't doing anything when the officer stopped him. "Was it because I took out my phone? Should I not have done that?"

"It's not your fault. And you didn't do anything wrong."

Jeremy eyed him briefly, but then turned away, staring at a line of ants zigzagging on the cement walkway and into the flower beds.

"Jeremy …" Michael paused. Jeremy kept his eyes on the ants. "There are things about this country that are messed up. One of those things is how some white people see and treat Black people. Stereotypes, the media, how it portrays us. I can't tell you the number of times I've been followed in stores or had people cross the street to avoid me."

"How can you stand it?" Jeremy asked. A tear rolled down his cheek.

"I can't stand it. But what I work hard to remember is who I am, that I am intelligent, kind, a hella good ball player" —Jeremy smiled— "and I don't let anyone take that from me. I don't let anyone define me but me. Knowing all that keeps me sane. But I also don't forget that there are a lot of people out there who see me as a threat, and so when I go out, every single time I go out, I remember that my goal is to make it back home."

"That sounds exhausting," Jeremy said, wiping the tears off his face.

"It is. It is."

Jeremy's eyes shifted to a mockingbird on top of a telephone pole cycling through its repertoire of songs. "You know what I had to memorize last week for social studies?"

Michael shook his head.

"We hold these truths to be self-evident, that all men are created equal, that they are endowed by their Creator with certain unalienable rights, that among these are life, liberty and the pursuit of happiness, blah blah blah."

"This country is a series of contradictions, Jeremy. The framers of the Constitution weren't angels. Heck, they were slave owners themselves. You do have the right to be treated fairly, to not have cops stop you on the street for no reason, to happiness and freedom." Michael paused. "Just because some people act all crazy doesn't mean those rights don't belong to you. But, you do have to be careful. You can want things to be a certain way, but you have to meet the situation as it is."

"Does it ever get easier?"

Michael was quiet for long enough that Jeremy turned and looked at him. Michael seemed to be watching the mockingbird now on a nearby pole. "Easier? Not sure if it gets easier. You just learn to armor up."

Michael faced Jeremy. "Jeremy, you need to understand. Some white people, like your mom, are allies and have your best interests at heart, though even allies can misstep and say things or do things that show they don't truly know what it's like to be Black. I mean, that's why she called me over. She knows she doesn't really know.

"But there are some white people that say they are allies but will stab you in the back when given the chance. They are the dangerous ones. And unfortunately you can't always tell who's who. That's why we tend to armor up. At the end of the day, we want and need to get home safely."

9. Following the Signal

"What was that all about?" Devon greeted Jeremy as he plopped down on his bed. He sat quietly for a moment before launching into the story of his morning. Neither Devon nor Sam said anything afterwards, and he was grateful, because he didn't want them to try and pretend to understand.

Birdbrain, however, couldn't help herself. "Untenable," she whispered to no one in particular.

"Shush," Devon whispered back.

Jeremy absentmindedly picked up his phone. "I almost forgot about the GPS. It seems to be working. Look." Jeremy held his phone out so they could see.

"So he's still at home. Um, actually he seems to be on the move." Sam pointed at the dot now moving on the screen.

"We need to have a plan," Devon said.

After several moments, Thing spoke up. "Wow, don't all talk at once."

Jeremy ignored him, but Sam said, "This always seems easy when it's in a book. You know, detective stories and such. They always seem so quick on their feet, and they're always in the right place at the right time."

"How do we get in the right place at the right time?" Jeremy asked.

"We know his other targets, or at least some of them, don't we?" Devon said.

Jeremy nodded.

"We could use the GPS to see where he's headed and based on the direction he's going we could try and get a head start. Perhaps we go into the city 'cause once there, we'd be closer to wherever he's going next."

"What do we do once we find him?" Sam asked.

"Let's figure that out on the way," Jeremy said.

"No, I think we need to have some idea of what we're going to do," Devon countered.

"Find him, get the hat and go," Jeremy said.

"What about the Christmas trees?" Sam asked. "In Paris you were insistent on making sure we took that tree back."

"Yeah, and look how that turned out," Jeremy said.

"Disastrous," Birdbrain quipped.

"I know," Jeremy said. "It was my idea to return the tree to it's spot near the Eiffel Tower last summer. Should have known he'd be expecting us."

"That would have been helpful," Thing said snidely.

Devon glared at Thing. "Yeah, but we did get the Eiffel Tower from him and at least had the hat long enough to restore the tower."

"True," Jeremy said, "but he ended up with the magic hat in the end."

"Regrettable," Birdbrain said.

"What is it with Birdbrain?" Sam asked.

"She's been studying the thesaurus," Devon said.

"Is that her new power or something?" Sam asked.

Devon burst out laughing. "Oh, I hope not."

"It is not my new power. I'm just trying to educate myself, you know, work my—"

"Birdbrain?" Thing cut in, chuckling.

Birdbrain clipped Thing over the head with her wing.

"If we can get the hat away from him, destroy it and avoid the loss of something as great as the Golden Gate Bridge, I think the city can deal with the loss of a couple of Christmas trees," Jeremy said.

"And the gingerbread house, sure. But what about the cable cars?" Devon asked.

"Oh, yeah. We should probably get those back." Jeremy perked up. "Do you know the inspiration for the cable cars?" he asked.

Devon leaned back against the wall and smiled. "No, but I'm sure you're going to tell us."

Jeremy smiled back at her. "Back in the late 1800s a man got the idea for the cable car after seeing horses being whipped when they struggled walking on the stone streets. I think they used the same cable system for mining."

"How do you know that?" Sam asked.

"I like doing research on the computer about random stuff I see."

"And that's more interesting than baseball?" Sam asked incredulously.

"Yep."

Sam chuckled. No one spoke for several moments. Sam broke the silence. "How are we going to get around the city?"

"We can use an electric scooter," Devon said.

"How?" Sam and Jeremy said.

"My dad and I used them up in Portland a few weeks ago. Jeremy, if you download the app on your phone, we can use the account my dad set up."

"Okay. Sam, can you bring a helmet from home?" Jeremy said.

"Helmets? Are you kidding me?" said Sam. "Why are you bothering about helmets?"

"Mom gave me a lecture once about wearing my helmet skateboarding. It's the law in California."

"Do you really think a police officer is going to bother us if we're riding a scooter without a helmet?" Sam asked incredulously.

Jeremy's eyes bore into Sam's, and a tension filled the now silent room. Devon shifted uncomfortably.

"Oblivious," Birdbrain muttered under her breath.

"I just got stopped for walking down the street, minding my own business."

Sam looked down at the floor.

Jeremy walked over and stared out his bedroom window.

"You'd just finished snooping around someone's house," Sam whispered.

Jeremy spun around. "I wasn't snooping! And I was invisible," he nearly shouted.

"Antagonistic," Birdbrain muttered.

Jeremy ignored her. He took a breath to calm down. "And it was extremely stupid," he said, no longer yelling. "I realized that part way through. But it needed to be done."

No one spoke for several minutes. Devon eventually broke the silence. "How about if today we go into the city and use public transport, see how it works? Then Sam can bring a helmet over tomorrow."

An awkward silence continued to hang in the air like thick fog on a San Francisco's summer day.

Devon tried again. "Jeremy, where's the car now?"

Jeremy picked up his phone. "Looks like he's stuck at the toll plaza. Devon, I know you said we need to have a plan, but I think we should get to the city."

"BART will take about twenty-five, thirty minutes. We could try and come up with a plan then," Sam offered.

Still not looking at Sam, Jeremy asked Devon, "What do you think?"

"Sure."

"Darn it," said Sam.

"What?" Devon asked.

"I always wear Giants' gear when I go into the city. Kind of a ritual- habit thing."

Jeremy was still frustrated. "Get over it," he snapped.

Sam chose not to respond.

"Awkward," Birdbrain said.

"Birdbrain, that's enough!" Devon admonished.

In the end they got a ride to BART from Jeremy's mom, after promising to check in every hour by text. Jeremy's mom gave him a big hug before they left the house.

Devon spoke up once they were on BART. "When we were in Paris, this man seemed to start small, and he saved the larger monuments for last, right?" Jeremy and Sam both looked at Devon. "Well, what if we assume he'd do that again? Then we could at least have a guess at where he'd be going next."

Jeremy nodded. "Okay. So that would mean the Golden Gate Bridge would be last and probably the Ferry Building before that. That would mean he would go for Coit Tower first."

"Or another cable car," Sam said.

"Well, let's get off at the Embarcadero," Jeremy suggested, "'cause we can walk to Coit Tower from there. Not sure how we can know which cable car he'd steal, there's so many. "

After departing the station, they headed down the Embarcadero as planned. They were sidetracked when Devon discovered that the loud birds flying overhead were parrots. Bright green and loud, they squawked as they flew over the road and settled in palm trees lining the street.

Jeremy texted his mom before checking the GPS. He stopped. "Guys, he's not coming this way."

10. Coit Tower

"What do you mean? Where is he?" Devon asked.

"He's driving down the Embarcadero in the other direction."

"What's down there?" Devon asked.

"The ballpark," Sam said. "Surely he's not going for the Giants' stadium. Oh, he better not be. If he …"

"Whoa, Sam," Jeremy said. "What's up with you?"

"What's up with … what do you mean? It's the Giants." Sam's voice grew louder. "You know, Willie McCovey, Juan Marichal, Orlando Cepeda, the Say Hey Kid, Willie Mays. There's a statue of Mays in front of the ballpark. Oh, he better not touch that."

Jeremy and Devon exchanged looks. Devon raised her eyebrows at Jeremy who shrugged.

"We've got to do something," Sam insisted.

"Sam," Devon said, "we can't try and follow this guy

everywhere. He's got a car, we don't. We have to stick to our plan of trying to head him off at Coit Tower."

"And what if he doesn't go to Coit Tower today?" Sam asked, scowling.

"Then we'll have to come up with a different plan," Devon said.

"What about these magic buddies? Can't we use them to help us track him?"

"We know where he is." Devon countered. "What would the buddies do if they got to him on their own?"

"I could steal the hat," piped up Birdbrain.

"You did that last time, and it didn't go so well," Devon said.

"No," corrected Sam. "She got the hat just fine in Paris. It's when I threw her again that she got caught."

"I think we need to stick together for now," Jeremy said. "At least until we have a better plan."

"And who's gonna come up with that?" Thing said from the side of Jeremy's leg.

"How about you, wise guy?" Jeremy said.

"Ok, I'd be glad to, seeing as your plan is to steal the hat and run," Thing said.

"Oh, and what's your plan?" Jeremy asked.

"Steal the hat and run … faster. Ha! No, just kidding. I think we should just wing it."

"Hey," said Birdbrain, "that's my line."

"What about you, H.D.?" Thing asked. "You gonna help us?"

"You bet. Let me at him, and he'll wish he'd never started this."

"Wow, that's a deep voice you got there, for such a small dog," Thing remarked.

"I'm only small on the outside," H.D. said.

"Clearly," Thing said.

"Okay, enough," said Devon. "What are we—?"

Sirens sounded in the distance.

All three of them looked at each other. Jeremy whipped out his phone.

"Whatcha—?" Devon started to ask.

"Twitter. I put in some hashtags to follow for news around the city, in case we wanted to … oh, Sam," Jeremy looked up in alarm, "you are not going to like this."

"What?"

"The statue of Willie Mays is gone."

Sam didn't say anything. His eyes were wide, and his face turned bright red.

"And," Jeremy consulted his phone, "the car is headed back down the Embarcadero, but he didn't get on the Bay Bridge, so he could be coming here."

"Maybe that was a diversion," Devon said. "Like when he stole the Venus de Milo at the Louvre, and then right after he took the Mona Lisa."

They were at the base of the Filbert Steps. Devon led the way up the stairs. Realizing Sam wasn't with them, Jeremy looked back. Sam hadn't moved but stood in the same spot, stunned.

"Man, he must really like those Giants," Jeremy muttered. "Sam!" he called out. "Come on."

The stairs were steep and endless. The surrounding houses hid behind trees and bushes providing a lush, green landscape, making it easy to forget they were in a city. Partway up, Devon let out a cry of delight. To their left were five parrots resting in a tree. "Oh, this must be Telegraph Hill!" she said.

Jeremy paused.

"What's the holdup?" Sam asked.

"Birds. Devon really, really likes birds."

"Yeah, I kind of figured that," Sam said.

"How?' Jeremy asked.

"Her shirts," Sam said.

Devon wore a blue t-shirt with a sketch of birds sitting on a telephone wire. Jeremy couldn't remember seeing Devon in a shirt that didn't have birds, so he'd stopped noticing.

"Okay, okay we can go." Devon peeled her eyes away from the parrots with apparent difficulty.

They continued upward, stopping several times to catch their breath. "I'm not sure we're going to get there in time," Devon said, after ten minutes of almost continual climbing.

Sam, Devon and Jeremy eventually reached the top of the stairs. They covered the relatively flat ground leading up to Coit Tower, while ignoring the view of the Golden Gate Bridge visible from the end of the parking lot.

"We need to get somewhere where we can watch the parking lot. If we're here, he'll see us," Jeremy said.

"How about we go up to the observation deck?" Devon said.

"Should we all go up?" Sam asked. "Wouldn't it be better to spread out?"

"You've got a point," Jeremy said. "What if one of us goes up, someone stays inside on the lower level, and one of us hangs out, say, over there?" Jeremy pointed to a clump of trees behind them that provided a view of the lot and the entrance to Coit Tower.

"Okay. I'll hang out in the trees," Sam offered.

"Do you mind if I go up to the observation deck?" Jeremy asked Devon.

"Go right ahead. I want to look at the murals inside. How much time do you think we have?"

Jeremy looked at his phone. "Maybe five minutes? I'd better get going." He walked up the short set of stairs and followed the signs to the gift shop where he purchased a ticket for the elevator to the observation deck. He passed Devon on his way to the elevator, viewing a mural of farm workers picking oranges. "See you in a bit."

"Right," Devon said.

Once he stepped out of the elevator, Jeremy walked up the two remaining flights of stairs. At the top, he ignored the amazing views and looked at his phone. The car was definitely headed toward them. He situated himself where he could see the road leading up to the tower.

"Pssst."

Jeremy glanced down at Thing. "What?"

"What's your plan?"

"What?" Jeremy asked, already having taken his eyes off Thing to watch the road.

"What's your plan? What happens when you see the car?"

"I don't know. Wait for him to come up here."

"What if he doesn't?" Thing said.

Jeremy looked down at Thing. His mind started whirling. What would he do? They were spread out but had no way of communicating. Jeremy had the only phone. He realized they hadn't thought this through.

Silently, he turned his gaze away from Thing, and a hint of blue caught his eye. He swore to himself, frustrated that he couldn't warn the others that the man was driving up to the parking lot. Now that the man was close, Jeremy didn't know what to do. He decided to stay put, hoping that the man would decide to come up the elevator. Though now that he thought about it, why would he? He didn't need to come up in order to steal the tower.

Jeremy swore under his breath again. He tried to find Sam in the trees but couldn't. His frustration mounted, and he tried to work some of it off by walking around the perimeter. Just before he reached the elevator, the door opened and the man, wearing the green newsboy hat, stepped. Jeremy abruptly turned around and walked the other way. "Can you make us invisible again, Thing?"

"I think so."

Jeremy unhooked Thing from his carabiner and held him in his hand. He waited for a moment until he thought no one was looking. "Okay, now."

Once invisible, Jeremy attempted to get close enough to swipe the hat off the man's head, but there were too many people. He needed to focus more energy than he wanted on not bumping into someone. The man didn't spend long on the deck, and Jeremy didn't have a good chance to grab the hat before the man returned to the stairs leading down to the elevator. His frustration mounted again and not paying attention, he bumped into someone.

"What the—?" The woman didn't finish her sentence as she looked wildly around for the person who bumped her.

Jeremy retreated quietly but couldn't find a good time to become visible without someone noticing.

A loud siren pierced the air; someone triggered the fire alarm. Tourists started heading down the stairs to the elevator. Jeremy brought up the rear, careful to keep some space between himself and the person in front of him. He stepped to the elevator. The door closed in his face. He forgot that he was still invisible, so no one held the door for him. Five minutes later, the elevator still hadn't returned.

11. Shrunk

Jeremy felt the building shake, hard enough that he almost fell over. After regaining his balance he ran back up the two flights of stairs to the top. He looked out over the side, but instead of the city, he saw the parking lot. And the cars were gigantic. Out of the corner of his eye he saw a hand reaching down. Jeremy ducked reflexively and fell over as the now miniature Coit Tower tilted on its side. Jeremy fell out onto the ground.

Jumping to his feet, Jeremy turned in circles, bewildered.

"Hey! Pick me up before I get stepped on!"

Jeremy grabbed Thing, now the size of a marble, and attached him to the carabiner hanging from a loophole of his jeans. "We need to find Devon and Sam." Jeremy realized the difficulty of this task. He seemed to be only about two inches tall, making it hard to see anything from a distance.

"What's that?" Thing stared up into the sky.

Jeremy looked up. Was that a bird? But they were too small. What if the bird thought they were edible? "Thing, we need to go invisible again, or that bird might eat us!"

"Nah, it's Birdbrain. Yoo-hoo, over here." Thing started jumping off of Jeremy's leg, only to be stopped by the carabiner.

Jeremy waved his arms and jumped up and down. Birdbrain landed next to them. "Hop on," she said.

"Can you take off on your own now?" Jeremy asked.

"I hope so."

Jeremy climbed onto Birdbrain's back and wrapped his arms around her neck.

"Well, this is cumbersome," Birdbrain quipped.

She started running and flapping her wings. She lifted off the ground and flew toward the trees where Sam hid before Jeremy went into Coit Tower.

"How did you know we'd shrunk?" Jeremy asked Birdbrain as he clutched tightly to her neck.

"I didn't. When Devon didn't see you leave the tower, she asked me to fly overhead to see if I could find you."

Luckily, there were not too many people around and those present were focused on the space where the tower once stood and didn't notice them flying overhead. Jeremy saw Devon and Sam through the trees. Birdbrain headed for them and landed in Devon's outstretched hand.

"Oh no! Jeremy!" Devon cried out. "What happened?"

"He shriveled," Birdbrain said.

"I did not," Jeremy said. "Birdbrain, words have context you know. I am not dehydrated."

"Oh, sorry."

"It's okay." Jeremy recounted his story to the others. Stunned silence followed, broken by a ping from Jeremy's pocket. He pulled out his cell phone. "Uh-oh, Mom just texted me." He stared at his phone for a moment and then typed in a response.

"Does that still work?" Sam asked.

"Huh?" Jeremy paused. The phone in his hand felt the same as before. His body did as well. When he pulled out the phone, he didn't consider that it might not work. "Yeah, seems like it," he said to Sam.

"What did you tell your mom?" Devon asked.

"That I followed a man with a magic hat, and when I forgot I was invisible, I got stuck at the top of Coit Tower and shrunk to the size of a LEGO character."

Devon's jaw dropped.

"I told her we were having a lot of fun and got distracted. What else could I say?"

"What are we going to do?" Sam said. "We have to get that hat back. Your mom will freak if she sees you like this."

"She'll freak? I think I'm freaking out," Jeremy said, trembling.

"Oh, Thing, you're so cute." Birdbrain chuckled.

"Not funny. That's not funny at all," Thing said.

"We have to get that hat." Devon glanced around at the parking lot which Jeremy could see from his perch on Birdbrain's back, was log jammed. People were standing in groups, ignoring those in cars trying to leave. "Jeremy, does your GPS still work?"

Jeremy checked his phone. "Yeah ... hey ... he's still here."

"What!" Devon and Sam exclaimed.

"I have to get into his car," Jeremy said.

He felt a kick at his side. "What, Thing?"

"You need to have a plan. Remember—"

Jeremy cut him off. "Yeah, yeah."

"What's Thing talking about?" Sam asked.

"I realized once I was up on the tower that I had no way to contact you guys once I saw the car come up the drive. You're right, Thing. We need to have a plan. But it's got to be quick. I have a cell phone so I can check in with my mom, but how can I get a hold of you guys?"

The three stared blankly at one another. "Are we assuming this man will go back to his house?" Devon asked.

The two boys stared at her. 'Well," she continued. "I think we'll have to. And if he doesn't, and you're in danger, Jeremy, at least you'll still be able to contact your mother."

"Oh, that would be a fun conversation." Jeremy noted Devon's impatience and added, "That's more of a plan than I've got." He paused. "Okay. He lives at 49th and Lawton. It's a mile from my house. Let's plan to meet there. Now, Thing and I need to get in that car."

"I think H.D and I should go too," Birdbrain said.

"I think that's a good idea," Devon said.

"Oh man ... I just got him," Sam said. "But, okay."

He unclipped H.D. "But where do I put him? Isn't he too big to ride on Birdbrain?"

"Uh-oh, there's his car!" Jeremy exclaimed. "We're not going to make it!"

"Put me down!" insisted H.D. He said it with such a deep, intense voice, Sam dropped him.

Before their eyes the small, stuffed Basset Hound turned into a full grown German Shepherd and took off running.

"What the—?" Sam started, but Devon cut him off.

"He's going to try and slow the car down. Birdbrain, get Jeremy over there."

Birdbrain flew off after H.D. who bounded ahead of them, running onto the drive, and causing the line of cars to stop suddenly. The man's car rear-ended the vehicle in front of him. Swearing, the man got out to assess the damage. Birdbrain took advantage of the situation and flew into the car through the open door. H.D., having succeeded in stopping traffic, ran around the car and jumped in, shrinking back to his original size and breed.

"Can you make us all invisible, Thing?" Jeremy asked as he grabbed Thing.

"Can I? Can I? How can you ask such a question?"

"Hurry, he's coming back!"

"Am I invisible?" H.D. asked in his small, Basset Hound voice. "How do I know if I'm invisible?"

"Thing! I thought you said—" Jeremy stopped mid-sentence, as the man was seconds away from getting into the car. "Get under there!" Jeremy hissed to H.D., who was not invisible. H.D. crawled under a jacket on the seat.

H.D. pulled his tail undercover just as the man got into the car. The vehicle rolled down the street and headed for the freeway. Twenty-five minutes into the drive Jeremy's phone pinged. The man turned and looked in the back seat, apparently having heard it, despite the volume being as soft as the phone was small. Jeremy quickly muted his phone before seeing his mom's text. He messaged her back immediately.

When the car stopped, Jeremy looked at the GPS on his phone to confirm that they were back at the man's house; he couldn't see out the window. The man got out of the driver's side and closed the door. Jeremy panicked; he couldn't figure out how to get out of the car. But the man opened the back door and reached to grab his jacket. Jeremy worried that H.D. would get found or that he, Thing and Birdbrain would get stuck in the car. When the man picked up the jacket, the seat was empty. Jeremy looked up and saw a bulge in one of the pockets.

"Birdbrain," Jeremy whispered, "we have to get out of the—"

12. Trapped

Birdbrain must have realized the danger they were in, because, still invisible, she flew out of the car before he could finish his sentence. She landed near the front door and waited until it opened, then scampered in. The man went into another room after throwing the jacket on the couch. Birdbrain flew to the sofa and quietly called out to H.D., who came out of the pocket chewing something.

"What are you doing?" Jeremy whispered.

"He had some leftover chocolate in his pocket."

"Dogs aren't supposed to eat chocolate," Jeremy said, distracted.

"Oh, we're not?" The deep voice of the German Shepherd gave way to the tiny voice of the hound. Apparently the hound was a rule follower.

"Wait, you can eat?" Thing said. "I didn't know buddies could eat. That is so unfair! Why did I have to be born without a—"

"Focus," Jeremy cut in. "We need to find the hat. Shush."

They didn't need to be told twice. The sound of footsteps grew louder before softening again. A door closed.

"H.D.," Jeremy said, "can you sneak into those other rooms, and see if you can find the green hat he wore in the car?"

"You bet." He took off and less than a minute later came back with a hat in his mouth. H.D. dropped the hat on the floor. "He left it on a chair. He's in the bathroom—"

"H.D.!" Jeremy hissed. "That hat is brown, I need the green one."

"Oh." H.D. picked it up, turned around and trotted into the back of the house. After he left, Jeremy glanced around and spotted a tablet with the heading: *National Policy Institute - goals*. Jeremy didn't have a chance to read further due to H.D. returning with a green ...

"A shirt H.D.? We don't have time for this. Come here." Jeremy, with Thing still in his hand, jumped off Birdbrain's back and onto H.D. who instantly became invisible. "Hide somewhere, Birdbrain," Jeremy said, before he commandeered H.D. into the back again. H.D. padded silently into a bedroom. A desktop radio played Top 40 music. Jeremy scanned the room, spotting the newsboy hat on top of the bed. Before he could point it out to H.D., a door opened, and Jeremy could hear footsteps approaching.

"Move, H.D." Jeremy hissed, "or he'll bump into us."

H.D stepped to the side just in time. The man froze in the middle of the room, his gaze moving from an empty chair, to a brown hat lying feet away on the floor. He turned slowly in a circle as if searching for something and Jeremy, noticing that the man didn't have a shirt on, realized he must be looking for the shirt still in H.D.'s mouth. The phone rang, and the man stepped to his desk to answer it, his back to them.

"Hello? Yes, this is Carl." He spoke loudly over the radio instead of turning the music down.

Jeremy ignored the rest of the conversation. "H.D. Where was that shirt when you found it?" His whispers were covered by the music.

H.D. dropped the shirt so he could answer. "Up on that chair."

"Well, go put it back … no. Put it behind the chair so maybe he'll think it fell off. Can you do that without—" but Jeremy stopped, because the moment H.D. dropped the shirt, it became visible, and the appearance of the shirt seemed to catch Carl's eye. "No, don't pick it up!" Jeremy hissed, but he was too late. The shirt was in H.D.'s mouth.

Carl stared at the spot on the floor where the shirt vanished, while someone tried to get his attention on the phone. "What? No … I mean yes … wait," and he turned around to write something on a piece of paper.

"H.D. Just drop the shirt, and let's get out of here," Jeremy said.

"What about the hat?" Thing asked. "Get the hat, H.D."

"What? No!" Jeremy hissed. But H.D. had already bounded up onto the bed. He grabbed the hat in his mouth. Luckily, Carl was still on the phone, but it sounded like he was about to get off.

"Go!" Jeremy whispered in H.D.'s ear. The dog bounded off the bed onto the carpeted floor which muffled any sound of his impact. As they landed, Jeremy saw Carl look at the shirt on the floor as he ended his call. Jeremy knew it wouldn't be long before he noticed the hat missing.

Out the door, down the hall and back to the couch. "Birdbrain, let's go. Oh crap, how are we going to open the door?"

"Are you crazy?" Thing exclaimed. "Use the hat!"

"I was going to wait but … " Jeremy jumped down from H.D. with Thing. "H.D., drop the hat on top of us … but not the—" The rest of his sentence was muffled. H.D. dropped the hat on Jeremy, upside down, smothering his words. It was dark and suffocating and for a split second, Jeremy panicked. H.D. must have realized his mistake, because he picked the hat up and placed it right side up. Jeremy wished with all his might that he and Thing be returned to their original size. A moment later he got his wish, but … "What?… Where did all these pizzas come from?"

There were six boxes of pizza stacked in front of them.

"I remembered you saying the hat gave the wearer any power they wanted," said Thing.

"And you chose to have pizzas appear? You can't even eat!"

"Yes, but the smell, oh, the smell."

Jeremy heard footsteps and burst into action. He scooped up the magic buddies, stuffed them in his pockets and grabbed the stack of pizza boxes off the floor. The door creaked slightly as it opened but closed without a sound. Jeremy walked quickly, unable to break into a run while balancing the pizzas. As he turned onto the sidewalk, a police car approached from two blocks away. His breath caught in his throat, the hairs on the back of his neck stood up, and he stopped for a moment. Not wanting to draw attention to himself, he forced himself to keep walking. One block away, the car slowed down. Right before the patrol car reached him, he heard someone call out his name.

"Jeremy!" Devon and Sam were running toward him. Devon tried to embrace him in a hug, but the boxes made it nearly impossible. Sam stopped as soon as he saw Jeremy. He bent over, hands on his knees, clearly winded. The police officer stared at Jeremy as the car came level with him, but then accelerated past. Jeremy breathed a sigh of relief.

"We need to get away from here," he said.

"Why ... do you ... have pizzas?" Sam asked, out of breath.

"Because it ends up that Thing's greatest desire is to be in a room filled with hot pizza he can't even eat."

Muffled sounds came from Jeremy's pockets. Jeremy handed the pizzas to Sam and Devon, freeing up his hands to pull the buddies out of his pockets. Buddies and pizzas changed hands until Birdbrain perched on Devon's shoulder, Sam hooked H.D. to his carabiner, and Jeremy did the same to Thing.

"I thought I told you before never to stuff me in your pocket again," Thing complained.

Jeremy remembered him making that request on the plane flight to Portugal the summer before last. "Yeah, well, I had to make sure we all got out of there, and I didn't want to risk dropping any of you."

"Oh, how thoughtful," said Thing sarcastically, apparently not ready to forgive having to smell the inside of Jeremy's pocket again.

Jeremy froze. He brushed his hand over his hair. "I dropped it."

"Dropped what?" Sam asked.

"The hat. H.D. dropped it over me which is why I'm back to my normal size. But in my rush to get out of the house, it must have fallen off. Thing, we have to go back."

"Go back?" Devon said. "Are you crazy?"

"You were just, you know … " Sam held his thumb and index finger inches apart.

"But Thing can make us invisible, and we are so close to the hat. We have to at least try. Come on, Thing."

"There you go again. I'm attached to you, you insufferable nincompoop. I kind of got to go."

"Back in a few," Jeremy called out as he ran down the street. Before he reached the corner, he slowed and looked around, making sure no one could see him. "Ready?" he asked Thing.

"Always. You? I'm not so sure."

"Yeah, whatever."

Jeremy—now invisible—approached the house as quietly as possible. He searched the ground hoping he'd dropped the hat outside but couldn't find it. Walking cautiously around the side of the house, he peered in a window.

Carl stood in his entryway, wearing his green shirt and a perplexed expression on his face. He sniffed the air, probably catching a whiff of pepperoni pizza. The hat was in his hand.

Carl looked down at the hat and understanding registered in his eyes. The moment before Carl put the hat on his head, something terrible occurred to Jeremy. The fairy tale they'd read in Paris said that the hat gave the wearer any power he or she wanted. Could one person keep changing his or her mind, gaining multiple powers? Right now could Carl wish to do something other than shrink objects? Or did the hat remember the wearer and limit each to one power?

Jeremy held his breath, while Carl put the hat on his head. Nothing happened, but Jeremy knew that didn't necessarily mean anything. Carl could have wished for something that Jeremy couldn't see. But then Carl shrugged, took the hat off his head, and placed it on a table.

Jeremy breathed a sigh of relief. It would appear that Carl's magical mischievousness would be limited to shrinking objects. At that moment, Jeremy couldn't think of a way to get the hat, and he felt uneasy about hanging around the house. "Let's go back."

"What? Are you kidding? We're so close."

"Keep your voice down, Thing," Jeremy hissed.

As Jeremy began this reprimand of Thing, Carl froze midstep—he was in the process of walking out of the room—then spun around. Clearly, he heard Thing.

"Oops," Thing whispered.

"Just don't move," Jeremy instructed.

They stood still as Carl stepped to the window, opened it—there wasn't a screen—and peered out, his head turning side to side. His arm darted out the window, right at Jeremy's head. Jeremy arched his back. Carl's hand missed him by an inch. A murder of crows in a tree overhead squawked as if each wanted to outperform the others. Carl watched them for a moment, then seemed to conclude that he had mistaken their vocalizations for voices. He withdrew his arm, shrugged and walked out of sight.

"Let's get out of here," Jeremy said, and this time Thing did not object. Jeremy's nerves were frayed. He wanted to get away from this house.

13. More Magic

Jeremy and Thing joined the others, becoming visible as they approached. Sam sat eating a slice of pepperoni pizza, and Jeremy's stomach rumbled at the sight. He grabbed a piece as he filled Sam and Devon in on his visit to Carl's house. After he finished, they sat in silence on the sidewalk eating, each lost in his and her own thoughts. Sam went to reach for another piece but he missed—the box moved. He reached again, and the same thing happened. Thing started giggling. Jeremy looked down at him and saw Thing watching Birdbrain.

"Are you doing that Birdbrain?" Jeremy asked.

Devon, staring off into some trees, presumably bird watching, turned back to the group and said, "Doing what?"

"Doing this," Sam said, reaching for the pizza box which moved just beyond his grasp.

"Well, you had three pieces and Devon and Jeremy each had one, and I thought it best you wait," Birdbrain said unapologetically.

"Wow, you can move things with your mind?" Devon asked.

"She better not move me," Thing said.

"You know what I mean," Devon countered.

"How far away can you be and still move something?" Jeremy asked.

"Not sure," Birdbrain said.

"Can you move big things like cars?" H.D., panting at the sight of the pizza, pulled himself together enough to ask the question.

"Will you all please stop using my name in a derogatory fashion!" Thing stood on the ground next to Jeremy, his oversized hands curled into fists at the sides of his round body.

Jeremy looked down at Thing and burst out laughing.

"Excuse you!" Thing sounded insulted.

"Sorry. It's just that you look so cute when you're mad." Jeremy curled his lips inward to try and keep from laughing again.

Ping. Jeremy received a text. "Oh man, I did it again. Can someone please help me remember to text my mom." He sent a message back to his mom, hoping it was enough to appease her.

"I thought you set an alarm." Devon grabbed a second piece of pizza before pushing the box toward Jeremy.

"I did, but then my phone went off when I was in the back of Carl's car. It wasn't very loud, but I think he heard it. I muted my phone after that."

"Oh, is his name Carl?" Sam said.

"Yep." Jeremy glanced at his phone. "We gotta go. I think I pushed Mom a bit too far today."

"You could just tell her you'd been magically shrunk to the size of the LEGO Spiderman you have hidden in your desk ... maybe she'd forgive you." Thing gazed innocently at Jeremy, but Jeremy knew it was payback for laughing at him earlier.

"I'm gonna have to put locks on all my stuff, aren't I?" Jeremy grabbed the last piece of pizza from the open box. "Let's take one of these," he said, indicating the stacked pizzas, "but Mom will ask questions if we show up with all of them."

Jeremy, Devon and Sam made it back to Jeremy's in record time. Jeremy hoped his quick return would keep his mom from giving him too hard of a time. She surprised him by being more relieved than upset. The three of them did have to help with dinner; spaghetti with sauce made from ground turkey, peppers, onions, mushrooms, canned sauce and a side of garlic bread. The extra pizza went in the fridge. After dinner they hung out in Jeremy's room for thirty minutes before Devon had to leave.

"Is anyone else suspicious about Mom not being more upset that I kept forgetting to check in?" Jeremy asked.

"Well, she knew we were with you," Sam said.

"Yeah, but you don't know my mom well enough. She is strict with a capital S."

"Do you think she knows something about the club, and what we're doing?" Devon asked.

"I'm not sure. Travis seemed pretty adamant that adults weren't part of the club, except for him and whoever is in charge." Jeremy paused as he watched Thing riding around the room on the back of H.D. "But remember, in Paris, when Mom and your dad, Devon, were tracking Heinke, that crazy 'I want to take over the world' lady?"

"Yeah," said Devon, watching Birdbrain fly above H.D. and Thing. "And Travis said they send our parents wherever we need to go. But what if they're working on the same problem we are, just from a different angle?"

"But they didn't seem to know about Carl, did they?" Sam said.

"No, that's true." Stumped, Jeremy decided to let it go. He watched the buddies cavorting around the room.

"But they do now," Devon said.

"They do now what?" Jeremy asked, distracted by Thing who held onto H.D.'s tail as he ran circles around the room.

"They've known about Carl since Paris. We could still be working on the same case."

That made Jeremy tear his attention away from the buddies.

"So, what's our plan now? Do we go back to the city tomorrow?" Sam asked.

"I guess we'll have to. It's frustrating," said Jeremy. We're no closer to getting the hat—"

"But you are close," said Thing as he did a handstand on H.D.'s back.

"What do you mean?" Jeremy couldn't help but be impressed by Thing's acrobatics. But also confused. Where did those arms come from?

"The guy lives within walking distance. That's close isn't it?" Thing pushed off H.D., did a somersault in the air and landed on his butt.

"True …" Jeremy's voice trailed off. Was he imagining it or did Thing have arms a second ago? He glanced at his buddy.

"What?" Thing asked, a glimmer in his eyes. But there were his big hands on tiny arms, just like normal.

Jeremy shook his head to clear it, trying to remember what he'd been about to say. Oh, yeah. "We can't just break into his house," he said. "We would end up in a whole heap of trouble." Jeremy frowned as he struggled to find a solution. Jeremy thought about being in Carl's house again. "Hey, I almost forgot. There were notes on Carl's table; something about the National Policy Institute."

"What's that?" Devon asked.

"No idea. But Mom didn't confiscate my phone so let's look it up." Jeremy typed into his search bar. "According to Wikipedia, it's a white supremacist organization."

"Is that who he's working for?" Sam asked.

"So both Heinke and this man Carl are working for far-right organizations? But why target Paris and San Francisco?" Devon asked. Answering her own question, she continued. "People who are racist are generally pretty homophobic aren't they? And San Francisco's known as being a welcoming place for gay people."

"Wait. Get a load of this." Jeremy scrolled down his phone and then back up. "It says here that while white nationalists have a history of homophobia, they are actually trying to recruit gay people through fear; they claim that people of the Muslim faith are terrorists who hate and kill gay people so gays and lesbians should want to rid the country of Muslims. Wow. That's messed up."

They were all silent for several moments.

Jeremy's mom knocked on the door before poking her head in. "Devon, it's time to go. We'll see you in the morning. We're all going to go into San Francisco tomorrow. And Sam, you and your mom are spending the night."

"Okay, be down in a minute," Devon said. As Jeremy's mom closed the door, Devon turned to the others wide-eyed. "What's that about?" she whispered.

Jeremy and Sam shook their heads.

"Well, see you tomorrow." Devon gave each boy a hug, gathered up Birdbrain and left to go downstairs.

Jeremy and Sam automatically went into the hallway and pulled out an inflatable mattress, pump and sheets and began setting up Sam's bed. Thing and H.D. were passing a tennis ball back and forth on Jeremy's floor. After going downstairs and saying good-night to their moms, Jeremy and Sam came back upstairs and got ready for bed. Jeremy became suspicious when Thing started giggling and sneaking glances at H.D. He pulled back his sheets and found the remains of a bag of pretzels at the foot of the bed.

"That's not funny, Thing."

"Maybe not to you." Thing snickered, and H.D. let out a soft chuckle. Sam joined in.

"Just you wait," Jeremy said to Sam. "If H.D. spends enough time with Thing, he's gonna learn a thing or two."

After Jeremy cleaned up his bed and the lights were out, Sam spoke up. "How are we going to try and find Carl if we're with our parents?"

"We're going to have to find a way."

"I could create a diversion," Thing suggested.

"I'm sure you could," Jeremy said.

14. Back to S.F.

The next morning, a Monday, Jeremy, Sam and their moms met
Devon and her dad at BART, wanting to avoid the hassle of driving
into the city. They packed into the train with commuters on their
way to work. Thing mumbled when they got off at the
Embarcadero.

"What's up?" Jeremy asked as they walked up the steps.

"That dude next to you, that's what. Not sure the last time he
showered."

"Remind me what we're doing?" Jeremy overheard Sam asking
his mom.

"Jess and Bob have a meeting here in the city, and we thought it
would be fun to make a day of it."

"Where's your meeting, Mom?" Jeremy asked.

"At an office on the Embarcadero. But it's not until later. Bob hasn't been to the Ferry Building, and he wanted to check it out."

"Who are they?" Devon asked, drawing Jeremy's attention to three drag queens who were wandering among the crowd entering and leaving the Ferry Building.

"Probably the Sisters of Perpetual Indulgence," Jeremy's mom said over her shoulder. "They do a lot of fundraising for various causes."

"Well, good morning, you fabulous beings." A six-foot tall sister greeted them with a smile. White makeup covered her face, and her lips were bright red. Yellow dots outlined her penciled-in blue eyebrows. She wore a nun's tunic; an overly large purple brooch decorated her white jester's hat.

"Good morning," the group replied.

"Can I interest you good people in our calendar? Sixteen months of beautiful sisters, and the proceeds help LGBTQ homeless youth."

Cheryl smiled. "Of course."

"Dad, can we get one?" Devon asked.

They walked away with two calendars and a group picture with the sister.

Once inside the Ferry Building, Jeremy, Devon and Sam broke away from their parents, promising to meet up later outside by the ferry dock. The crowded building made conversation difficult. They went outside to the back, where they could almost touch the bay.

Devon walked up to a railing separating the walkway from the water, leaned against it and stared out at the bay. Jeremy breathed in the salty air and followed her gaze. A brown pelican dove into the water. Sam wrapped his arms around himself, shivering. A layer of fog hung over the bay.

"Remember when Travis said that Heinke's group wanted to cause panic that could lead to markets crashing and destabilization across Europe?" Devon said.

Jeremy nodded remembering Heinke's speech about wanting to restore world order. He still remembered the spite in her voice.

"What if Carl's group is trying to do something similar, using one minority to attack another," Devon continued. "It doesn't seem like he was working with Heinke's group. But what if they want to cause panic and maybe blame the disappearance of Coit Tower and …" Devon paused. Her face blanched. "... this Ferry Building." Devon's voice raised half an octave. "What if the Ferry Building is next on his list?"

Jeremy understood Devon's worry about another San Francisco monument disappearing; especially one they were standing next to. "I thought about that," Jeremy said. "I think I should go small again."

"What!" Devon and Sam chorused.

"How else are we going to get into his house and get the hat?"

"I'm sure we can think of something else," Devon said incredulously.

"But we know that I can return to my normal size with the hat, so what's the danger?"

"What's the danger?" Devon stared at him, disbelief etched on her face. "Are you kidding? There's so much that could go wrong. You could be seen, or stepped on, or … or eaten by a stray cat—" Jeremy looked at her incredulously—"and that's before you even get into the house."

"Do you have a better idea?" he asked flippantly.

"Do *you* think this is a good idea?" Devon turned on Sam, her voice seeping with accusation.

Sam took a step back from Devon. "This is the first I've heard of it."

Devon spun to face Jeremy. "Jeremy, we need to slow down and try and think this through a bit more."

Jeremy didn't know why he felt so irritated. He couldn't figure out another way to get the hat from Carl, and once he thought of this idea, he couldn't let it go.

"Weren't we trying to figure out why a white nationalist group would target San Francisco?" Sam asked, clearly trying to keep the peace. He wouldn't look at Devon, focusing, instead, in the direction of two seagulls fighting over a scrap of food on a bench.

"White nationalists aren't the most rational thinkers," Jeremy said. He turned away from the seagulls. "They're extremists, and so is their thinking. First of all, they don't just hate Black people. They're against anyone who isn't white or straight."

"What makes you say that?" Sam asked, focusing once more on his friends.

"Since we discovered that Tech monitors hate groups, I've been trying to learn more about the far-right." Jeremy's voice lost some of its edge.

"But that still doesn't tell us why they're targeting here," Sam said.

"I guess what I'm saying is with people who are that radical, what makes sense to them, might not make sense to you or me," Jeremy said.

"Maybe it's just a target of opportunity," Devon said.

Both Sam and Jeremy looked at her, puzzled.

"Well, Carl lives in Oakland. Maybe he got tired of traveling and decided to attack somewhere closer to home."

"Huh," said Jeremy. They stood in silence, turning to look out over the bay. Several pelicans were diving into the water. Seagulls mulled around near their feet, pecking at crumbs on the ground.

"Do you think your parents are working on this case, too, just from a different angle?" Sam asked, breaking the silence.

"Possibly.… I wonder. What are the chances Travis called this meeting to ensure we were able to get to the city?" Jeremy said.

Devon shrugged. "Oh, here they come."

Their parents came out of the Ferry Building, and they all watched as a ferry pulled away from the dock.

"We're going to head over to our meeting," Jeremy's mom said.

"Okay." Jeremy accepted a side hug from his mom. "How long will you be?"

"A couple of hours."

"Mom," Sam asked, "what are you going to do?"

Cheryl laughed. "I'm guessing you're hoping it's something that doesn't involve you."

Sam smiled and had the courtesy to look apologetic. He accepted a full hug from his mom.

"I'll leave you kids to yourselves. Let's meet back here in two hours, so at one o'clock." Cheryl handed Sam some money, and the other parents did the same.

"Try to find something healthy for lunch," Jeremy's mom said.

Jeremy smiled and nodded as he accepted the money from his mom.

15. Shrunk Again

After their parents went their respective ways, Jeremy, Devon and Sam went back into the ferry building to get some lunch, all agreeing to try the Mexican restaurant. The smell of black and refried beans and salsa made Jeremy's mouth water.

Over lunch, they struggled with developing a plan. Devon wanted to check out the cable car turnaround at either Powell street or the Fisherman's Wharf, convinced that Carl would strike there, grabbing another car when it was empty. Sam wanted to check out the Giants' stadium to see or not see the missing Willie Mays statue for himself. Jeremy wanted to stay near the Ferry Building, convinced it was Carl's next target.

"What if we jump on Muni and head down to the stadium?" Sam suggested, leading the way out of the restaurant. "On the way back we can get close to the Powell Street cable car turnaround, check it out, then head back here."

"I'm staying here," Jeremy said defiantly, before following Sam outside. "I'm not going to pretend we can plan exactly when Carl's going to make his next move. Besides, maybe it's better if we spread out."

"Are you kidding?" Devon glared at Jeremy. "The last time we split up you shrunk so small a bird could have eaten you for lunch."

Jeremy couldn't help smiling at the bird reference. It was always about birds with Devon. He leaned against the rail separating the walkway from the water.

"Stop it," Devon snapped at Jeremy. "It's not funny."

"What do ya think, Birdbrain?" Thing asked. "Do you think Jeremy would make a tasty snack?"

"With or without his clothes on?" Birdbrain giggled.

"What? No, we are not talking about this!" Jeremy said indignantly. Sam doubled over laughing, and Devon broke into a grin. "Okay, ha ha," Jeremy said. "But can we be done now?" The buddies continued to chuckle.

"I still don't think we should split up," Devon said.

"I hear you, Devon," Jeremy said, "but wandering around the city when there's a good chance he's going to end up here doesn't make sense to me."

"Okay," Sam said. "I'll admit. There's nothing to be gained from checking that he took the statue at the ballpark. I don't see why Carl would go back there, anyways."

"Devon. Remember, he already stole two cable cars. Do you really think he'll try for more?"

"Okay, okay," she said. "Let's all stay here. But I don't think you should go small, again. It's too risky."

Jeremy avoided her gaze.

An alarm went off in the Ferry Building. Jeremy spun around and watched as people streamed out of the building. He locked eyes with Devon. She seemed to be pleading with him as she shook her head, but he couldn't resist the impulse to act. Jeremy smiled, shrugged and ran back toward the Ferry Building.

"Jeremy, no!"

Jeremy ignored Devon, weaving through business people with their midmorning coffee and confused tourists to get to the doors. He saw security personnel directing people to the exit, and he skirted around them, hiding behind a fruit display. Soon, the building emptied. Jeremy made his way as quietly as possible to a pole near the entrance, large enough for him to hide behind. The same feeling he'd experienced when Coit Tower shrunk came over him. Jeremy reached out for the pole, almost too wide to hold onto, knowing that he might fall over when Carl, he assumed it would be Carl, picked up the building.

Sure enough, the building rose up into the air but stayed fairly level. Jeremy couldn't see Devon or Sam but he saw H.D. bolt out from the crowd straight at Carl. H.D., in his ferocious form of a snarling German Shepherd, jumped up at Carl, putting his paws on Carl's chest. As Carl tried to fend off the dog with one hand and hold the miniature Ferry Building with the other, Birdbrain flew toward Carl. A moment later she flew away, the hat in her talons.

Jeremy's heart sank. In that moment, he realized the stupidity of his plan, of his impulse to do something, anything, instead of waiting for a better opportunity. Devon and Sam managed to get the hat, while he stood, stranded, the size of a miniature action figure, in the shrunken Ferry Building still in Carl's hand.

"Jump!" came Thing's tiny voice from his side where he remained tethered by the carabiner clip.

"What? But it's too … we're too small." Jeremy didn't want to be stuck with Carl now that he didn't have the hat, but at his size, the ground was too far away. Plus, what if someone stepped on him?

"Aim for H.D.," Thing said. "H.D. Hey, H.D."

H.D. stopped bothering Carl once Birdbrain retrieved the hat. Steps away and retreating further, he must not have been able to hear Thing.

"He's not gonna like this," Thing said.

H.D. stopped suddenly, bouncing backwards as if he'd bumped into an invisible wall. Jeremy smiled, despite his circumstance. Thing gained the power to throw up invisible barriers when they were in Paris. If his situation wasn't so dire, he might have laughed, for H.D. attempted to walk forward three times in a row before finally turning back toward Carl.

"H.D.!" Jeremy yelled.

While Jeremy caught H.D.'s attention, he also attracted Carl's, the latter lifting the miniature Ferry Building up to eye level. Before it reached that height, Jeremy grabbed Thing in his hand, and they both became invisible. Jeremy could see Carl's eye, a freaky sight, staring into the building, searching for the source of the voice. Apparently giving up, Carl lowered the Ferry Building just as H.D. came bounding back.

Still invisible, Jeremy jumped, falling what felt like three stories onto H.D.'s back. Jeremy had to let go of Thing to grab tight to the dog with both hands.

"Go H.D. Go," cried Jeremy.

H.D. tore through the crowd with Jeremy hanging on for dear life. The dog reached the edge of onlookers when—

"Stop H.D." Jeremy's legs flew up in the air. For a moment he was in an involuntary handstand position, H.D. stopped so suddenly. Jeremy's legs dropped down, and he sat up assessing his options. His mom and Devon's dad were standing with Devon and Sam.

"Over there, near that statue of the man by the ferry terminal, hide behind there."

H.D. ran behind the statue of Gandhi.

"Why are we hiding?" Thing asked. "I can make us all invisible."

"Oh right, I forgot."

"You forgo—?"

"Not now Thing," Jeremy said. "I need to figure out a plan.... H.D., can you get me up onto the base of this statue?"

H.D. put his front paws on the base, and Jeremy scrambled up before peering around Gandhi's foot. The crowd around the area was massive. Apparently word was out about the Ferry Building, and people were coming to see for themselves. Jeremy searched for Devon and Sam.

"H.D., can you—" Jeremy started.

"Incoming!" Fear in Thing's voice made the hair on Jeremy's neck stand up.

The Travelers Detective Club

16. The Ferry Building

A seagull dive-bombed Jeremy and Thing. Jeremy grabbed hold of his buddy, who didn't need to be told what to do, going invisible immediately.

"Can birds smell?" Thing asked.

"Oh god, I don't know." Jeremy dived under the toes of Gandhi's left foot which were elevated slightly. "H.D., scare it away!"

"How?"

"How? Act like a dog!" Jeremy crouched down, trying to make himself smaller, and inched as far back as possible under the statue. Several birds flew overhead. Two alighted on the base of the statue. "Bark at them, whatever, I don't care."

H.D. jumped at the seagulls, barking. He chased after one.

"What's he doing? H.D., come back!" he yelled. "Stupid dog."

"I'm going to tell him you said that," Thing said.

"Oh, did I say that out loud?"

"Uh-huh."

"Yeah, well, he's left us here."

"You did ask him to act like a dog," Thing said. "But luckily, his barking caught Devon's attention. Look."

Devon ran out of the crowd toward H.D. It took her a moment to get his attention, but she must have, eventually, because H.D. led her back to the statue.

"Jeremy! Jeremy! Where are you?"

Jeremy let go of Thing. "Under Ghandi's foot."

"What are you doing under there?"

"The seagulls thought he'd be a tasty snack," Thing said.

"If they got me, they'd get you too, wise guy," Jeremy said. "Do you have the hat?"

"Right here."

"Hold out your hand," Jeremy said. He stepped onto Devon's palm.

"This is so weird," she said, lowering him to the ground.

"How do you think it is for me?"

"I told you—" Devon started.

"Put the hat on top of us, quick," Jeremy said.

"Devon? What are you doing?" Devon's dad approached from the opposite side of the statue.

"Just do it, Devon," Jeremy said.

Jeremy sat down as the hat rested on top of him. He made his wish, and he and Thing returned to their normal sizes just as Devon's dad walked up. Jeremy pulled off the hat and popped up off the ground, startling Devon's dad.

"Oh hi, Jeremy. We wondered where you were."

"Right here." Jeremy gave an awkward smile. His right hand behind his back, Jeremy stuffed the hat into his pocket.

"Devon, what were you doing, chasing a stray dog?" her dad asked.

She shrugged. "I thought it had a pigeon in its mouth. You know how I love birds, Dad."

Jeremy tried not to laugh. He spotted H.D. out of the corner of his eye, hiding behind the statue, having returned to his small, Basset Hound self. Jeremy stepped sideways, reached down and grabbed him, stuffing him into his other pocket while out of view of Devon's dad.

"Devon, you know better. Don't let me see you doing that again."

"I know. You're right. I won't, Dad." She turned her head away from him as she spoke, the corner of her mouth turned up in a partial smile.

"Let's get back to the others. Jeremy, your mother is worried about you."

"She's always worried about me."

Devon's dad led the way back toward the crowd.

"What did you tell them?" Jeremy whispered.

"Nothing," Devon said. "They'd just found us when I saw H.D."

"Oh, Jeremy, thank goodness." His mom grabbed him once he was within arm's distance.

"What's up Mom? I'm fine. I just wanted to get away from the crowd."

"Well, okay. But let's get out of here. This reminds me of Paris. How can a building just disappear?"

As everyone started walking toward the BART station, Jeremy grabbed Devon's arm and whispered, "Sam!" They both stopped and looked at Jeremy. "We can't leave. Carl has the Ferry Building. What are we going to do? Just go home and have dinner?"

"You want to tell your mom that?" Devon said.

Jeremy glared at her.

"I know, I know," she said. "You're right, but—"

"Kids, what are you doing?" Cheryl called back to them.

"Devon, come on," her dad said.

As they caught up to their parents, Jeremy's mom's phone rang. She stopped walking to focus on her call.

"Oh. I almost forgot." Jeremy pulled H.D. out of his pocket while his back was to the adults. "Here, Sam."

"Whew. That was awful," H.D. complained. Sam clipped H.D. back to the carabiner hanging from his belt loop.

"Yep, his pockets are nasty," Thing said.

"Mr. Davis needs us back at the office," Jeremy's mom said.

"How long are you going to be?" Jeremy asked.

"I don't know. But I think you should come with us. I don't want you wandering around right now."

"Mom, but why? What do you think will happen?"

"A building disappeared, not people," Sam added.

"Sam!" Cheryl said sternly. "Don't you dare talk back to another adult."

The group stood still, making people walk around them.

"Ms. Johnson." Devon addressing his mom this way caught Jeremy by surprise. Devon's dad flashed her a warning, but she continued. "What if we promised to check in every thirty minutes and be back as soon as you asked us to?"

"I think it best if you all come to the office while we see what Mr. Davis needs. If we're going to be awhile, then I'll consider other options."

The other adults murmured their agreement. Recognizing defeat, Jeremy, Sam, and Devon followed their parents down the street.

"Hey, I forgot these things changed colors," Sam whispered. He was just behind Jeremy and Devon. "What does purple mean?"

Jeremy and Devon stopped, both turning to look at Sam and then their buddies, who were purple.

"Let's stay close to our parents for now," Devon said, hurrying to catch up to the adults.

"But what does it—" Sam said.

"It means we're in danger," Jeremy interrupted. Jeremy looked over his left shoulder. He didn't see Carl but picked up his pace, following Devon. "Come on," he said to Sam.

H.D. let out a low growl. Carl was twenty feet away, to Jeremy's right. Jeremy met his gaze. Devon and Sam closed around Jeremy, the hat still in his back pocket.

Thing kicked Jeremy's leg. "Watch this," he whispered. Carl bumped into an invisible wall and fell down backwards, a paper bag slipping out of his hand.

"Incoming," Birdbrain said as the paper bag slid on the pavement over to them.

Devon bent over and picked up the bag. "How did … is that … Did you do that?"

"Remember the pizza box?" Sam whispered.

"Oh, right," Devon said.

"Are you kids okay?" Jeremy's mom called over her shoulder.

"Yep," Jeremy answered. Luckily, they reached their destination at that very moment. Devon's dad opened the door to let them into an office building. They all scooted inside.

"Excuse me," a voice said from behind them.

Jeremy ignored it and kept walking.

"Excuse me. Those kids have my bag."

Jeremy's mom, along with the other adults, turned around. At the same time, something knocked against Jeremy's leg while Devon gasped.

"Excuse me?" Devon's dad said.

"That girl took my bag."

"What bag? I think you must be mistaken."

Devon no longer had the bag in her hand and Thing was invisible. Jeremy realized why his buddy suddenly felt heavier.

Carl came closer, too close. Devon's dad stepped between Carl and Devon. "As you can see there is no bag, and I suggest you leave my daughter alone." The two adults stared at each other. Devon's dad's piercing stare met the malice in Carl's eyes, before the latter turned away.

"Come on kids," Jeremy's mom said. They headed toward the elevators.

"The nerve of that guy!" Devon's dad started. "Wait a second. Wasn't that—?"

Jeremy's mom cut him off. "Bob." Her voice held a warning.

Jeremy's mom and Devon's dad exchanged a glance. Jeremy watched the adults have one of those conversations adults seem to have, the quiet kind they don't want the kids to hear. The ding of the arriving elevator caught everyone's attention. The ride up to the fifteen floor was a quiet one. Jeremy didn't dare glance at the others, and he hoped Thing would think to stay invisible. They exited the elevator, turning left down the hallway. Devon's dad opened the fourth door on the right, and they all followed.

"Kids, wait here," Devon's dad ordered, indicating the waiting room.

After the adults left, Sam sat down in a chair. "Wait. Why did my mom go back there?"

"And it seems your mom and my dad recognized Carl," Devon said to Jeremy.

"Well, we know Tech monitors far-right extremist hate groups." Jeremy, like Devon, remained standing.

"What if we're all working on the same case after all?" Devon said. "And if so, why can't we tell our parents?"

"Because." Travis stood in the doorway. "They can't know about the magic."

"Speaking of magic." Thing appeared at Jeremy's side. "Tada." He held out the bag to Devon who took it.

"Thanks."

"Don't you think, now that buildings are disappearing, that they might begin to realize that something magical is making all this happen?" Sam asked.

"You'd be surprised, Sam," Travis said. "Adults will go to great lengths to avoid seeing what is right in front of them."

"Well, is there any harm in telling them?" Devon asked.

"Telling us what?" Devon's dad walked up behind Travis, unnoticed by them all. "And Devon, where did you get that bag? Is that Ca—that gentleman's bag?"

Devon looked down at the bag in her hand as if she'd forgotten it was there. "This … no … it … someone just handed it to me."

"Who?" her dad persisted.

"Me," Jeremy said.

"And where did you get it?"

"Um … " Jeremy started lamely. He had no idea what to say and as the seconds ticked by, he became more and more uncomfortable. It was as if someone turned off his brain.

"See we were walking," Sam said in a rush of words, "and this man was chasing after us, so Thing, that thing on Jeremy's belt," Sam gestured to Jeremy's side, "magically threw up an invisible barrier to make him fall over. When he dropped this bag, Birdbrain, over there—he pointed to Devon's side—made the object slide across the pavement to us. And inside that bag is the miniature Ferry Building."

17. Magical Pizza

Silence followed Sam's outburst. Jeremy's mouth hung open. Devon stared in disbelief at Sam. Her dad stood, shell-shocked, his eyes moving to the magic buddies who were hanging, limp, from their carabiners.

"Huh? Very funny, but really. Where—"

Travis stepped in. "I gave them the bag. I thought they might be hungry so I brought some snacks from the breakroom. I hope that's okay. I know I should have asked you first."

"Oh, that's fine," Devon's dad said. He seemed to have forgotten Sam's outburst already. "I just came to say we're ready for you."

As Devon's dad held the door open for Travis, he addressed the kids. "We're going to be a couple of hours. All the parents …" He stopped mid-sentence. "Are you kids okay?"

Jeremy realized his mouth was still hanging open, as was Devon's. Sam wore a curious expression, a mixture of disbelief and amusement.

The three shared a glance. Jeremy recovered first. "Yeah ... yeah," he stammered. "You were saying?"

Devon's dad looked from one kid to the next, puzzled, but quickly moved on. "Yes. I was saying we agreed that as long as you check in every thirty minutes, you can head outside."

They stumbled out their thanks before hurrying out the door.

"What," Jeremy rounded on Sam, "was that about?"

"I don't know.... You froze, no one else was saying anything, and Travis just finished telling us that adults don't believe what's right in front of them. So ... I went with the only thing I could think of—the truth. And it seemed to work."

"How can they be so blind?" Jeremy said.

"Travis is right," Sam said. "Adults really don't or won't recognize magic."

"Even when it's right in front of them," Devon said, opening the bag. "Well, it's here, the Ferry Building."

"What do we do with it?" Sam asked.

"I can use Thing," Jeremy said, hitting the down button for the elevator. "He can make us both invisible, and we can replace the Ferry Building and use the hat like we did in Paris."

Devon and Sam murmured their agreement while they rode the elevator down to the first floor. "Wait," Devon said, just as they were about to exit the building. She looked down at Birdbrain. "Okay, they're not purple, but we need to expect that Carl will be out there somewhere, waiting for us. Jeremy, why don't you and Thing take the bag and go invisible now, just in case Carl is watching."

"Great idea." Jeremy accepted the bag from Devon, and grabbed his buddy in his hand.

There was no sign of Carl as they headed back toward the empty site of the Ferry Building. The walk was awkward, because Devon and Sam kept cutting Jeremy off or bumping into him. They approached the area from the side, keeping on the edge of the crowd of roughly one hundred, gathered to observe the now vacant lot. Yellow caution tape prevented onlookers from getting too close.

Jeremy left Devon and Sam and continued past the security tape and police officers. He placed the miniature Ferry Building in what he hoped was the correct spot. Knowing he'd have only seconds from the moment he placed the model to when people would notice it, he put it down and ran away from the area to ensure he wouldn't be smashed. Pulling the hat out of his back pocket, he put it on his head and wished for the Ferry Building to return to its original size in its original space. Nothing happened.

Jeremy panicked. He tried a second time but nothing happened. A police officer noticed the building and started to approach. Jeremy pulled the hat off his head, worried it might fall, sprinted to the model and picked it up. As quietly as possible he returned to the spot he'd left Devon and Sam. He tapped Devon on the shoulder. "It's me."

"What happened?"

"I don't know. I put the hat on and wished for the Ferry Building to return to its original size and place just like you did."

"Wait. You've used the hat before, right?" Sam said.

"Yeah … when I needed to return to my regular size after I shrank."

"Well, maybe you only have the power to return yourself to your regular size but not anything else."

"Glad I chose the power of pizza," Thing said.

Jeremy ignored Thing. "Then Devon, you do it."

"What about you, Sam," she asked. "Do you want a turn?"

"Well—" Sam started.

"No," Jeremy interrupted. "We may need you to use it for something else."

The others agreed. After looking around to make sure people nearby were focused on the empty lot, Jeremy handed Devon the hat and Thing, making him visible once more while Devon disappeared.

"Wait, what about a diversion?" Sam said.

"What do you mean?" Devon said from Jeremy's side.

"Well, the cop that saw the building when you put it down, Jeremy, keeps glancing at the spot as if waiting for it to reappear. I'm worried Devon won't have enough time to get away from the area and do the magic."

"Any ideas?" Jeremy asked.

"Pizza," Thing said.

"Not now, Thing," Jeremy said.

"What do you mean, not now? Who doesn't like pizza?"

"He has a point," Sam said.

"I'd like some pizza," H.D. said.

"Devon," Jeremy said, "what do you think? … Devon?"

Jeremy craned his neck, trying to find Devon despite knowing it was impossible. In front of a yellow line of caution tape, behind which a throng of people stood, a pile of pizza boxes suddenly appeared.

"Free pizza!" Devon's voice rang out as the boxes slid off the pile and along the ground so that pizza boxes were scattered across fifty feet of caution tape. Those near the front of the crowd went crazy, grabbing at the pizza, so that multiple people were tugging on each box.

"Wow, people do love free pizza," Sam said.

The police stepped in to try and restore calm. Jeremy focused on the center of the lot and sure enough, the miniature Ferry Building appeared. Moments later, screams rent the air as the Ferry Building returned to its original size. Devon appeared at Jeremy's side a moment later. Handing over Thing, she said, "What now?"

"We need to figure out how to get the other stuff from Carl." Jeremy pulled out his phone to check his GPS and there were two texts from his mom. "Oh no, I'm … we're in so much trouble."

"What?" Sam said.

"We didn't check in." Jeremy frantically texted his mom. "We need to get back." He started running; the others joined him.

"Not so fast." Carl stepped in front of them. "Give me the hat."

Jeremy took a step back, moving between Carl and Devon who peeled the hat off her head and held it at her side. Carl came at them, but a deep growl emanated from Sam's side, and H.D. stepped in front of the group. His full-sized German Shepherd self, H.D. bared his teeth and snapped at Carl.

"Excuse me, officer." Carl tried to get the attention of a police officer standing with his back turned, some distance behind Jeremy's group.

"Oh crap." Jeremy's shoulders tensed.

Carl stepped to the side away from H.D., addressing the cop now walking further away from them. "Officer!" he called out louder.

The officer turned around.

"These kids have an off-leash dog that's trying to attack me."

Jeremy held his breath, the tension moving to his chest. He took a step back.

As the officer approached Carl, Sam scooped up the now miniature H.D. and stuffed him in his pocket.

"What dog?" the cop asked.

Carl whipped his head around, and then turned in a complete circle, confusion and astonishment on his face.

"Actually," Devon said, her voice shaking slightly, "this man is harassing us. We're late meeting our parents, but he keeps blocking us from leaving."

Jeremy tried to remember to breathe.

"They're lying," Carl said.

"Do you know this man?" the officer asked the group of three.

They all shook their heads.

"Can we go?" Devon said.

"Yes, of course," the officer said, rounding on Carl.

Jeremy followed Devon and Sam away from the scene, erupting in nervous laughter when they were well out of sight. "That was brilliant, Devon."

"Yeah, it was," Sam added. "Can you be that quick on your feet when our parents start to yell at us in a couple of minutes?"

That wiped the grin off Jeremy's face. "My mom may not let me go out again. I always forget to check in."

"Why don't we tell them the truth, at least part of it?" Devon said.

Sam looked as confused as Jeremy felt. Devon seemed to realize this. "We'll tell them that we were distracted by the return of the Ferry Building, and if that's not enough, we can add that Carl confronted us."

Jeremy started to interrupt, but Devon talked over him. "No, we won't use his name. And remember that our parents seem to know who he is."

18. Sam's Turn

Back at the office, Devon, Sam and Jeremy did not get the response they expected. Their parents were all just glad to see them. "But I thought you were mad," Jeremy said to his mom. "I always forget to check in."

She smiled. "You didn't realize the time when I texted you, did you."

His confusion must have shown on his face. "I asked where you were not because you were late but because all of a sudden we saw the Ferry Building appear and heard a lot of screaming."

"Oh. Okay. Can we go back out then?"

"Um, no."

Jeremy shrugged. "Can't blame me for trying."

"Dad," Devon said, "are you going to be long?"

"Yes, unfortunately, it may be a couple of hours."

"Well, then, can Jeremy, Sam and I head back?"

"Back where?" he asked.

"Back to Jeremy's," she said.

Jeremy tried to make eye contact with Devon, but she seemed to be deliberately avoiding his attempts. Why? And why did she want to go back to the East Bay when Carl was in San Francisco? Oh … right. "We'd rather hang at the house," Jeremy said, "than here in the office."

"Wha—?" Sam started but Devon cut him off with a glare.

"How will you get home, Jeremy?" his mom asked.

"We can take BART and then walk or call for a ride."

"With how crazy it is, I'd rather call you a ride from here. I don't want you wandering around anymore."

"What do you think is going to happen to us?" Jeremy said.

"You can stay here in the office or take a ride back to the house. Your choice." Her tone told Jeremy it was not up for discussion.

"We'll take the ride."

"Thanks, Ms. Johnson," Devon said.

Jeremy thought it suspicious that his mom wouldn't let them leave the building until she received a text that their ride was outside, waiting for them. It ended up that the others had the same thoughts.

"But remember," Devon said, "while they tried to hide it, they seem to know who Carl is. Perhaps they think he's dangerous—"

"— seems like he is," cut in Sam.

"... and," continued Devon, "they just want to keep us safe and away from him."

"Good thing they don't know we're going to his house," Jeremy said as he stepped into the rideshare car.

"What?" Sam said.

Devon gazed at Jeremy before nodding. "If Carl is in San Francisco, that means he's not at his house," she said. "It will give us a chance to look for Coit Tower, the cable cars, and the statue of Willie Mays."

"And the Christmas trees," added Jeremy.

"Are you kidding?" Sam turned in his seat and looked straight at Jeremy. "I thought we already talked about that being a bad idea."

"Atrocious," Birdbrain quipped.

"What?" Sam said.

"Awful, dreadful, lousy," Birdbrain said.

Jeremy knew he shouldn't care about the trees. But he didn't like the idea of not getting everything back from Carl.

"So breaking and entering, huh," Sam said, after tearing his attention away from Birdbrain.. "Haven't you been lecturing me on keeping you out of situations where you might be profiled? And now you're thinking of breaking into someone's house?"

"That's why I'm going to do it," Devon said.

"What?" Sam and Jeremy chorused.

"Let me have Thing so I can be invisible—"

"Take H.D. too," Sam said.

"Yeah, but don't ask him to find anything," Thing added.

Everyone looked at Thing. "What? Last time he retrieved the wrong hat and then grabbed a shirt. Almost got us caught."

"Mistaken," Birdbrain cut in.

"What?" Thing turned on Birdbrain. "I'm not mistaken."

"Not you, him," Birdbrain indicated H.D.

"Well, you ordered pizza," H.D. countered.

"It was good, though, wasn't it?" Thing said.

"Wouldn't know. No one saved me a—"

"Guys, cut it out." Jeremy noticed the driver peering at them from his rearview mirror.

Twenty minutes later, after the driver dropped them off at Jeremy's house, his mom having given strict orders to the driver, the three headed over to Carl's address at a jog. Once near the house, they stopped to catch their breath.

"Um, how do you plan on getting into the house?" Sam asked Devon.

"Carefully?" Devon's voice betrayed her uncertainty and fear.

A police car drove around the corner. The policeman looked at them as he drove past.

"Or you could walk through the front door," Thing said.

"What do you mean," Jeremy asked.

"He just pulled into the driveway," Thing said.

Everyone turned to face the house, watching as Carl got out of his car and went into his house.

"That changes everything," Devon said.

"Is it true that the hat gives us any power we want?" Sam asked.

"I think so. Why?" Devon asked. "Do you have an idea?"

"What if I used the hat to see into the house, to look for the tower and statue?"

"Like x-ray vision?" Jeremy said.

"Wow, could you see inside bodies?" Thing asked.

"Ewww, no thank you," Devon said.

"You could use the hat to shrink him," H.D said.

"Or to make him freeze," Birdbrain added.

"That'd be cool," Sam said. "Have a miniature Carl running around trying to stop us as we search his house."

"No, it's not," Devon said. "If the hat only gives us each one power, who would unfreeze him, or make him normal size again? No, I don't think we should use the hat to do anything to a person. And I'm having second thoughts about going into his house, especially with him there. If we get caught by him or the police we're in big trouble. No, I think we need to come up with a new plan."

As Devon spoke, two cars pulled into Carl's driveway and two additional vehicles parked along the street. Six men walked up to Carl's house.

Sam grabbed the hat from Devon's hand. "Can I borrow Thing?" he asked Jeremy.

"Sure." Jeremy unclipped Thing and handed him to Sam.

"Wait," Devon insisted. "What are you doing?"

"I have an idea." He smiled at Devon but didn't say more and instead turned and ran toward Carl's house.

"Sam! Come back!" Devon cried out. She took several steps as if to give chase.

"Devon, chill out," Jeremy said. "What are you worried about?"

"What am I worried about?" She looked at Sam's retreating profile then back at Jeremy. "Haven't you noticed that Sam can be a bit impulsive?"

Devon must have taken Jeremy's quizzical look on his face for a "no."

"Throwing Birdbrain ... tackling Carl in Paris."

"Okay ... yeah ... but tackling Carl turned out okay."

Devon glared at Jeremy. "There are six men in there plus Carl. How does this turn out okay?"

"Well, then let's go stop him."

"Why do you think I started after him?"

Jeremy ignored Devon's glare and ran toward the house with her on his heels, but Sam was already out of sight.

They slowed down as they came to the garage, separated from the house by a sloping patch of lawn. Jeremy tapped Devon on the shoulder, pointed to the back of the garage and headed that way. They rounded the corner, Jeremy hoping he would find Sam or get some bright idea of what to do. But they ran into a fence just behind the detached building. As Jeremy sighed and turned to go, something in his peripheral vision caught his eye. He stepped back and peered into the side window of the garage.

"Devon, check it out." Jeremy stepped away so Devon could have a look.

Devon peered into the garage. She turned back to Jeremy, her eyes wide with shock.

"I know, right?" Jeremy said. "Let's see if we can get in."

Jeremy reached for the door next to the window but the knob wouldn't turn. "Well, that would have been too easy. You wouldn't know how to pick a lock, would you?"

"Um, no," Devon said.

"Ugh! Being this close and not being able to get in is so frustrating!" Jeremy complained.

"Maybe I can help."

"What? Who? Is that you Sam?" Jeremy turned around in a circle. "Where are you?"

A chuckle broke the brief silence.

"Thing," Jeremy scolded, "show yourself."

Sam and Thing appeared inches from Jeremy who stepped back, startled. "Ha, ha, very funny."

"I thought so," Thing quipped.

"What'd you find out?" Devon asked Sam.

"That I should be more careful when I make an important wish."

"What do you mean?" Jeremy said.

"Well, I had this great idea for a magic power—freeze people momentarily, so they'd unfreeze on their own, see. So we wouldn't need to use two different powers."

"That sounds good enough," Jeremy said. "What happened?"

"I was at the door with the hat on, invisible. I realized that if I opened the door everyone would notice. Also the door was locked. So I thought to myself that I wished I could get in the door without anyone noticing me, and when I touched the doorknob, the door swung open just enough for me to squeeze through, and no one noticed. But then when I tried to make everyone freeze nothing happened, and I realized I'd used up my one wish. Three men stood near the entryway, and I worried that I would bump into one of them, so I just turned around and left."

"He panicked," Thing said.

Sam glared at Thing. "No one asked you."

"Well, it so happens you picked the absolute best magic power," Devon said.

"How ya figure?"

"Look in the window," Jeremy said.

Sam peered in the window, then turned back to Jeremy and Devon, his eyes wide.

"Mind using your new power to get us in there?" Jeremy grinned.

Sam grinned back.

19. Cornered

Taking the hat from his hand and placing it on his head, Sam grabbed the knob and turned it, opening the door.

An ear splitting siren rent the air. All three kids froze, shocked expressions on their faces. Devon spoke first. "Grab the tower, cars and statue and let's get out of here."

Sam grabbed them, stuffed them in his pocket and headed out the garage door. Jeremy stepped in and grabbed two objects off of an enormous train table and raced after Devon. At that moment, the back door to the house opened and several people poured out yelling obscenities.

Jeremy grabbed Thing from Sam. "Guys, grab hold of me."

"What?" Sam and Devon exclaimed.

"Can you do it, Thing?" Jeremy asked.

"I don't know. I'll try."

"Just grab my arm," Jeremy instructed the others.

Just as several men, including Carl, came around the side of the building, Jeremy and the others inched behind the garage into the small space between it and the wooden fence. Jeremy held his breath as Carl's face appeared around the corner, staring directly at them. But it worked; Thing managed to make them all invisible. The three stayed still until the voices and footsteps retreated back to the house. Devon and Sam let go of Jeremy. Still holding Thing, Jeremy peered around the corner. The coast was clear.

"We need to get out of here," Sam said.

"Okay, grab hold of me again and let's go," Jeremy said.

Devon and Sam got on either side of Jeremy, and they each grabbed an arm. "Okay, Thing, let's go invisible again." Jeremy started walking forward but …"

"Jeremy, stop!" Devon cried.

"What?" But then he saw what. Neither Devon nor Sam were invisible. "Thing?"

"I'm sorry, but it's too much," Thing said.

"Uh-oh," Sam said.

Jeremy looked down at himself and saw his body come in and out of view. "Perhaps if I give you a moment to reset …"

"We need to get out of here," Devon said, worry etched on her face.

"We can't walk by the house," Sam said. "They'll see us."

"Over the fence, we have to go over the fence." Jeremy indicated the fence behind the garage.

"But we don't know what's behind there." Devon walked up to the fence and peered through a space between the boards. "I can't tell."

"Probably another house," Sam said.

"How about I take a look," Birdbrain said from Devon's side.

Devon stared down at Birdbrain for a moment. "That's … brilliant." She unclipped Birdbrain and gently tossed her in the air. Birdbrain flapped her wings, dropped slightly before flying over the fence. Before they could miss her, she returned. "Well?" Devon said.

"Can't go that way." Birdbrain landed on Devon's outstretched hand. "There are people back there."

"What are we gonna do, then?" Devon said, as Birdbrain rustled her feathers.

"Should we just run for it?" Sam asked.

The three of them stared at each other. Jeremy could see fear flitting in Devon's eyes. He understood why. It would be easy enough for someone in the house to see them and dart out the front door after them.

"Hey, Birdbrain," Thing said. "Can you still move stuff?"

"Right," Devon said. "Maybe Birdbrain, you could provide us some cover."

A voice called from inside the house. "I'm gonna check out back again," and the sound of the back door opening sent chills up Jeremy's spine.

"We have to run for it!" he said, and not waiting for the others, he took off. He could tell from their footsteps on the gravel that Sam and Devon were close behind.

"Hey!" a voice called out from behind them.

The front door opened and three men came pouring out of the house, not twenty feet away. Jeremy couldn't help looking over his shoulder and at that moment, a brick flew through the air and hit the leg of the man nearest Sam, who sprinted even with Devon. The man landed with a thud, tripping those who were right behind him.

As they rounded the corner, Jeremy saw a car coming up the street that made him bristle. Instinctively, he grabbed Thing. "Please tell me you can go invisible." Looking down, Jeremy couldn't see his body. "Sam, Devon, stop running! There's a—"

"I see it," cut in Devon.

"Sam, give me everything, including the hat."

Sam started to put his arms out front.

"No, behind your back. Okay, got them. I gotta go."

"Why—" Sam started but Devon cut him off.

"Sam, are you still asking those questions?"

Jeremy saw Devon give Sam a look of incredulity, and Sam's eyes widened in understanding. Jeremy took off running down a side street, still clasping Thing in his hand. Once he reached the next corner, he stopped and looked back. A police officer was talking to Devon through his window. As Jeremy tried to slow his breathing, he saw Devon wave, and the officer drove off.

"Down here, guys," he called out. Devon and Sam looked his way and started walking toward him. Feeling safe, Jeremy hooked Thing back on his carabiner hanging from his jeans and let go. Jeremy took two steps toward his friends when the men from Carl's house came charging around the corner. "Oh crap, they don't look happy. Thing, can you—"

"Devon and Sam are in the way," Thing said.

"Move over," Jeremy yelled, waving his arms to indicate they should move onto the street.

Devon stepped off the curb into the street, but Sam stopped. Devon grabbed him and pulled him off the sidewalk, the men feet away. Before the closest man could grab Sam, he and then the others hit Thing's invisible wall and fell backwards onto the sidewalk. All three kids ran and didn't stop until they got to Jeremy's house.

They stood out in front of the house, bent over at the knees, gasping for breath. "Maybe we should get inside, just in case." Devon peered at the others, as she leaned on her knees.

"Good idea," Jeremy said, while Sam nodded.

They hustled up the front steps and into the house. Jeremy led the way, and hearing voices, he put his index finger to his lips, while looking over his shoulder. Devon closed the door without making a sound.

"... Policy Institute members just met," Devon's dad said. "But a source says it was interrupted. There was a break-in at the house."

"Hey, kids. There you are." Cheryl walked into the living room from the downstairs office. The conversation in the kitchen stopped.

Jeremy's mom burst out of the kitchen. "Where in the blazes have you been?"

"Um ... out?" Jeremy said, immediately hanging his head, because he knew he'd just given the wrong answer.

"Upstairs, young man," his mom ordered.

"See you," he muttered to the others before trudging upstairs.

Up in his room, Jeremy emptied his pockets onto his desk before flopping on his bed. He knew he'd blown it, and that his mom would be disappointed. The front door opened and closed twice. His mom's footsteps sounded on the stairs. Jeremy bolted upright, reached his desk in two steps and swiped the miniature figurines into his desk drawer. He sat back on the edge of his bed.

His mom knocked before coming in.

"I'm sorry, Mom. I know I blew it."

"Ya think?" She held his gaze until he looked down at the floor. "What were you thinking?"

Jeremy stared at his feet. When he looked up, his mom stood in the same place, arms crossed, watching him.

"I wasn't, I guess. I just seem to lose track of time."

"Weren't you instructed to come straight home from the city? That's why I got you that ride."

"We did come home." His mom tilted her head disbelievingly.

"We did. I'm serious. But then we went back out again."

"Where?"

"Around." His mom glared at him. "Around ... around the neighborhood.... Isn't that allowed?" Jeremy tried to keep his voice conciliatory.

"What happened the last time you went 'around?'" his mom said with air quotes.

"What? I was by myself." Jeremy's voice rose. "And so now I can't ever go out? Even with friends?"

"Of course you can go out," his mom said exasperatedly. She walked over and sat on the bed next to him. "But when I send you home from what I think is an unsafe situation, I expect you to stay home."

"What was unsafe about the sit—" Jeremy almost used air quotes to say, "situation" but caught himself. "—about what happened in San Francisco?"

"It doesn't matter. What matters is you not following my instructions."

"I'm really sorry, Mom, I am." He looked directly in her eyes as he apologized, before his eyes found the floor again. "But I didn't know we were supposed to stay home once we got back. I thought you just didn't want me taking BART." He glanced at his mom, and her eyes softened which encouraged Jeremy, so he kept going. "I guess I need to make sure I really understand—"

"Okay, now you're laying it on a bit too thick," his mom interrupted.

"Okay, I'll stop." Jeremy grinned sheepishly, and his mom wrapped her arm around his shoulder, giving him a side hug. "But seriously. Are you never going to let me go out on my own again?"

"Of course not. You have to live your life, but we also need to keep you safe."

"Maybe you could get me another t-shirt."

"What do you mean?"

"Remember. You bought me a shirt that said, 'Don't Touch My Hair,' 'cause white people couldn't seem to stop touching my head when I was younger?"

His mom chuckled.

"So maybe there's a t-shirt that says, 'I'm just a kid,' or 'I'm just walking,' or …. I don't know." Jeremy shrugged.

His mom playfully rubbed his head. "I have to go into the city for work again tomorrow."

Jeremy looked at his mom hopefully.

"What?" she said. "You want to go into the city again?"

Jeremy nodded.

"Why?"

"We were having fun, but then we had to leave early." Jeremy wracked his brain for ideas. "Devon was so excited when she saw parrots, and she wanted to go see them on Telegraph Hill, but we didn't get a chance. And she's never been to Pier 39." Jeremy didn't usually plead, but he felt desperate.

"So you want another chance ... again."

Jeremy smiled and nodded.

"Under one condition."

Jeremy waited.

"You need to set an alarm on your phone every hour so you remember to check in."

"Why didn't I think of that?"

"Because you're thirteen, that's why."

"I'm almost fourteen."

"Great. Then I can expect you to be more responsible, can't I?"

"I just walked into that, didn't I?"

"Yep." His mom smiled, gave him one last hug and got up off the bed. "Come down in a few and help with dinner."

"Okay," Jeremy said. "And Mom?" His mom turned around, her hand on the doorknob. "Thanks." She smiled and left the room.

20. Surprised

The next morning found Jeremy, Sam, Devon and their parents on BART, having waited for the morning commute to die down. After ensuring that Jeremy set an alarm on his phone, and knowing where they were going—Telegraph Hill and Pier 39—his mom and the other adults allowed the kids to go off again.

"How in trouble were you?" Devon asked.

"Enough," Jeremy said. "You?"

"Same," Devon said. "What about you, Sam?"

"Yep," Sam replied. "I'm actually surprised they let us go out again."

"Me too," Devon said. "Just to be sure, I've set the alarm on my watch to go off a couple minutes after your alarm, Jeremy."

"Good idea," he said. Jeremy glanced at the others. "So, ready to finish this?"

"Yep," Sam and Devon chorused.

"We're headed to put the tower back, right?" Devon said.

"Yep. Just make sure you say something about the parrots because that was the excuse I used for coming back to San Francisco, that you wanted to see them up close."

Devon smiled. "Perfect. 'Cause that's what I told my dad, too. What excuse did you give, Sam?"

"Funny enough, I didn't." They all stopped. "My mom just said she was going into the city with your mom," he said looking at Jeremy, "and that I was to hang out with you guys." Sam started walking again and the others followed.

"Why would your mom get involved, Sam?" Devon asked as they headed up the Filbert Street Steps. "What does she do anyways? For work I mean?"

"She's a computer programmer. She has the week off for the holiday. Maybe she's trying to help or something."

They were all quiet for the next several minutes as they concentrated on hiking up the stairs. Once they were in sight of their destination, they stopped to catch their breath and hatch a plan.

"Any ideas?" Sam said.

"I could walk it back ..." Devon said, her skepticism apparent in the hesitancy with which she spoke and the look on her face.

"Well, it did work last time," Sam said.

"True ..." Devon's voice fell away.

"What?" Jeremy asked.

"I'm not sure I want to try that again. It was only thanks to Thing's pizzas that we got away with it."

"Hey, let's use the buddies," Jeremy said.

"Oh, finally," Thing said. "I thought you'd forgotten us, again."

"Nah, you're too much of a pain in my butt to forget," Jeremy said.

"I'd like to kick you in your—"

"Guys!" Devon said.

"Yeah, Thing," Jeremy chuckled, "listen to Devon."

"Fffttt!"

"Love you too," Jeremy said.

"I can do it," Birdbrain said.

"Yeah?" Devon said.

"Just get it close enough, make sure there aren't any barriers around, and I'll do the rest."

Jeremy and Devon started walking, when Sam called out.

"Wait, guys. How do we know Carl isn't around, waiting for us like he was in Paris?" Sam asked.

"Good point," Devon said.

"Okay. So, let's make sure we're ready for him." Jeremy unclipped Thing and handed him to Devon." He also handed her his backpack with the hat and other figurines. "Go invisible with Thing, and don't walk next to us, just in case."

"Now, that sounds like a plan," Sam said. "But, wait."

Jeremy and Devon stopped again, turning back toward Sam.

"Where are we going to meet, after it's done?" he asked.

"How about back here?" Jeremy said.

"But what happens if Carl's there, and he chases us? We don't want to lead him toward Devon or vice versa."

"Okay, then," Devon said. "Let's have two spots. Here and ..." her voice trailed off, apparently out of ideas.

"... the dock behind the ferry building," Sam said.

"That works," Jeremy said. "And Sam, you and I should walk up first, check out the situation, and Devon, you can follow behind us."

"Sure, just don't give it away that I'm behind you, in case anyone is watching."

Jeremy nodded. "Good luck." He turned and walked with Sam toward the Coit Tower parking lot. A handful of cars waited for their owners, who lingered on the edge of yellow caution tape, staring at the empty space. As the boys walked toward the small group of gawkers, someone grabbed Jeremy's arm.

"Hey!" Sam exclaimed, for someone seized him as well.

Two men Jeremy recognized as part of the group from Carl's house the previous day were pulling Jeremy and Sam away toward a car parked off to the side, a distance from the crowd and other cars. As Jeremy struggled, he glimpsed Sam unclipping H.D. A moment later, a snarling German Shepherd barked and lunged at the men, causing them to loosen their grip on the boys enough for them to wrench free. As the men were trying to dodge H.D., cries erupted behind them, and Jeremy turned to see Coit Tower standing in its rightful place.

"How in the ...?" one of the men called out.

"Sam! Let's go!" Jeremy ran toward the stairs with Sam hot on his heels. Out of the corner of his eye, Jeremy saw a bizarre site. An electric scooter headed down the hill, but there appeared to be no one driving it. Jeremy immediately stopped and turned around, bumping into Sam. Bending over, grasping his forehead, Jeremy tried to steady himself as his head pounded.

"What are you doing?" Sam asked, from his position on the ground. He must have seen the scooter, because he said, "Oh."

"Send H.D."

Sam got the idea. After putting him on the ground, H.D. bounded toward the two men as they stepped into their car. H.D. got in between one of them and the car door on the driver's side.

"Get away! Go!" The man kicked at H.D. H.D clamped his jaw onto the man's foot and stepped backward, causing the man to fall to the ground. The second man, having jumped into the passenger seat, emerged from the car, a gun in his hand.

"H.D.! Watch out!" Sam yelled. H.D. must have sensed danger because his legs and chest turned purple. He disappeared from sight.

"Where? What? Where did that dog go?" the man said, looking from side to side.

The man on the ground jumped up and said, "Who cares, let's go." Both men jumped into the car and took off out of the parking lot.

"H.D.!" Sam yelled, jumping up from the ground and running toward the spot where he'd last seen his buddy. Jeremy followed close behind. They found H.D. on the ground in his Basset Hound stuffed form.

"How did you get away?" Sam asked.

"I felt myself change colors, heard you yell, and figured I better disappear. I switched back and crawled under the car."

"That was brilliant!" Sam said.

"And now we need to get out of here," Jeremy said.

Sam clipped H.D. to the carabiner hooked on a loop of his blue jeans, and both boys took off running for the stairs. They scrambled down, skipping the last two steps of each flight, jumping to the landings. They ran down the street but soon slowed to a walk, as they again ran out of breath.

"What time is it?" Sam asked.

"No idea. Why?" He glanced at Sam, but before Sam could say anything, Jeremy stopped in his tracks. "Oh no!" He realized that they must have been gone at least an hour, and he hadn't checked in with his mom. He went to reach for his phone in his back pocket but it wasn't there. "Crap, now I've lost my phone."

"Let's just get back to the Ferry Building and find Devon," Sam said.

"Did you see her … or I mean, not see her riding that scooter?" Jeremy said, starting to run again.

"Crazy, right?" Sam said.

Neither talked until they got back to their meeting place, saving their breath. They walked back and forth along the promenade behind the building, looking for Devon. After two times back and forth they stopped. Five minutes in one place and Jeremy started pacing; ten minutes and his heart raced, fifteen and he imagined various scenarios, and they all included him being grounded. Finally, after twenty minutes they saw Devon roll up on a scooter.

"There you are," Jeremy said, running up to her. "Where have you been?"

Sam came alongside Jeremy.

"I went down the Embarcadero and replaced the statue of Willie Mays at the Giants' ballpark. Only, I'm not exactly sure I put it in the right spot, but it will have to do."

"That's awesome, Devon!" Sam exclaimed.

"And I put the cable cars down on a track. It will probably clog up traffic but I figured it was the safest thing to do.

"Good thinking," Jeremy said. "Um, we have to get to the office … I'm so busted." Jeremy shook his head.

"Why?" Devon asked.

"I lost my phone and never checked in."

Devon pulled Jeremy's backpack off her shoulder, unzipped it and pulled out a phone. "You left it in the backpack." She smiled at the look of incredulity on Jeremy's face. "Good thing, too," she added. "I was able to use the app you downloaded the other day to unlock the scooter up by Coit Tower…. You probably should have a passcode for your phone."

"That's great," Jeremy started, "but we still—"

"And I texted your mom to check in."

Jeremy breathed a huge sigh of relief. "Wow, Devon. I—"

"Tell me what happened after I left," Devon said.

Jeremy and Sam took turns filling her in on H.D.'s narrow escape and their race back along the waterfront.

"I don't know about you," Devon said, "but I've had enough excitement for one day. And I don't want to chance running into those guys again. How about we head back to the office?"

Both boys agreed. On the way they laughed and joked, relieved they managed to do so much.

21. Holiday Planning

Wednesday afternoon, Devon's mom flew in from Portland, and everyone spent the day at Jeremy's. While the adults planned for the next day's feast, the kids hung out upstairs. Jeremy and Sam tried to get Devon interested in a video game but with little success.

"What's the point?" she asked.

"You build stuff, like buildings or cities. And then your friends can come check it out," Jeremy said.

"That's a lame explanation," Sam said.

Jeremy turned on Sam. "Ok, wise guy. How would you describe it?"

Devon interrupted. "So, it's like LEGOs but on a screen."

"Kind of," Sam said.

"Like I said, what's the point?" Devon said.

"Just try it," Jeremy insisted.

"Ok. If I try it, then you have to watch something with me."

"Sure," Sam said.

"Um, Sam," Jeremy said, "do you know what you just agreed to?"

"What?"

"Okay," Devon said before Jeremy could answer, "show me what to do."

Jeremy smiled while Sam launched into his explanation. Fifteen minutes later, Devon gave up, bored, and chose to watch the boys play. Not much later, she put an end to their game. "Okay, it's your turn to watch something with me."

"Here we go," Jeremy said.

"What are we watching?" Sam said expectantly.

"May I?" Devon said, indicating Jeremy's computer.

"Go ahead," Jeremy said.

Devon typed in the search engine and soon enough, a documentary on birds appeared on the screen. Birdbrain, playing cards with Thing, flew over and landed in front of the computer.

"Birdbrain, you're blocking the screen." Devon picked her up and put her on her shoulder.

"Are you serious?" Sam said.

Jeremy chuckled, but Devon's glare stopped him.

"Why do you like birds so much?" Sam said.

"They're beautiful, they can sing and they can fly. Isn't that amazing?"

"Yes." Birdbrain said. "Aren't we amazing?"

"Since when can you sing?" Thing asked from the floor, a building made of cards rising next to him.

"Shush," Birdbrain said, "I want to watch."

***

"We need to destroy the hat," Devon said by way of greeting when she opened the door to Jeremy's room that Thanksgiving morning.

"Yeah, but not before we replace these." Jeremy opened his desk drawer and pulled out two miniature Christmas trees.

"You didn't," Devon said.

Jeremy grinned.

"Oh yes, he did," Sam said. "But after what happened in Paris?"

"They were on the train table, in the garage. I couldn't help it," Jeremy said. "Okay, maybe I could have. I guess I could just keep them for decoration, but we could also return them on Friday, and then destroy the hat."

"My mom mentioned wanting to go to Ghirardelli Square which is close to Pier 39," Devon said.

"And I'm sure we could convince our parents to go for a walk across the Golden Gate Bridge," Sam said.

"Why the bridge?" Jeremy asked, puzzled.

"Dropping the stones and medallions off the bridge seems a good way to ensure they won't be found again," Sam said.

"We can't throw things off the bridge!" Devon said incredulously. "That's illegal, not to mention littering."

"We won't throw them. We'll just … drop them," Sam finished sheepishly.

"Sam's got a point," Jeremy said. "They're powerful magical objects. We need to ditch them somewhere they won't be found again."

"How about we decide about that later and figure out how we're going to return the trees?" Devon said.

"Sure, okay," Jeremy said. "Only, I'm not sure we'll be able to return both of them."

Sam and Devon looked at Jeremy. "Well, we'd have to go to different parts of town. I don't see our parents traipsing all over San Francisco or letting us wander that much."

"They might if we suggest we all take a cable car," Devon said. "I've never taken one, and I'm not sure my parents have either."

"Me neither," Sam said.

"Really?" Devon said.

"It's one of those things locals do when family and friends come to town," Jeremy said. "Which is probably what everyone else is thinking of doing the day after Thanksgiving. The lines will be awful."

"Maybe not if we go early," Sam said.

"Oh right. Your mom is almost as bad as mine about getting places early," Jeremy said. "Maybe we can use that to our advantage for once."

***

"Hey, Mom," Jeremy said. "Can we go into the city and ride the cable cars tomorrow? Devon's never been."

Everyone sat around the dining table, finishing dessert: pumpkin and apple pie with ice cream and/or whipped cream. Jeremy chose both pies and both toppings.

"It's a crazy time for that, Jeremy," his mom said. "The Friday after Thanksgiving is the busiest shopping day of the year."

"We thought you kids would want to just relax tomorrow," Devon's dad said.

"Dad," Devon chimed in, "I thought you wanted to go on the cable cars."

"Yes, well …" His eyes shifted to glance at Jeremy's mom. He straightened up in his chair. "I think a nice, relaxing day here would be best."

"But—" Devon started.

"Maybe you're right," Jeremy interrupted.

"What?" Devon said.

Jeremy ignored Devon's attempt to catch his eye. "Perhaps we can have a movie marathon."

"That's a great idea," his mom said a little too enthusiastically, while Devon's dad nodded his head.

Later, up in Jeremy's room, Devon rounded on him. "What was that about? Why did you give in so easily?"

"Yeah," Sam added, "I thought you wanted to ... what?"

Jeremy's grin seemed to surprise the other two. "Guys, relax. Of course I want to ... clearly our parents don't want us to go into the city. And I want to know why."

Devon flopped down on Jeremy's bed. "So what do you propose?"

"I'm not sure. But I thought it might be a give away that we were up to something if we kept insisting on riding the cable cars. I've never expressed any interest in going on them before."

"Oh, oh, oh. Can we go on another nighttime flight?" Birdbrain flapped her wings and rose up off the bed only to be stopped by her carabiner clip.

Devon chuckled. "Birdbrain, we can't do that every time."

"But I missed it last time."

"I know. But ... I'm sorry."

Birdbrain turned her back on Devon.

Devon threw her hands up in the air and silently appealed to Jeremy and Sam.

Jeremy shrugged and Sam apologetically shook his head, but then his eyes got big.

"Jeremy, can I borrow Thing?"

"Sure."

"Why don't I ever have a say in who does what with me?" Thing complained.

"Thing," Sam said, "will you come with me for a minute?"

"Sure." Thing bounded onto Sam's hand as if nothing was wrong.

"Really, Thing!" Jeremy said, shaking his head but smiling. "You are too much, sometimes."

"Only sometimes?" Birdbrain said. "Thing, you're slacking."

"Guess so. I'll need to step it up from now on."

With Thing in his hand, Sam turned toward the door.

"Where are you going?" Devon asked.

"To spy on our parents." Sam grinned, and silently slipped out the door.

"Crafty," Birdbrain said.

Jeremy and Devon stared at one another after Sam left. "How come I didn't think of that?" Jeremy said.

Devon shrugged. "At least Sam did." She unclipped Birdbrain and tried to pick her up, but Birdbrain flew to the other side of the room.

"Hey, Birdbrain," Jeremy said.

"Yes?"

"It's nighttime, and you just flew."

Birdbrain glared at Jeremy and turned her back.

Moments later Sam entered the room.

"What did you find out?" Jeremy asked.

"Not much. They mentioned the National Policy Institute, and they seemed confused about what the group planned to do next. They seemed to be stuck on the meaning of a particular code word."

"What code word?" Devon asked.

"Tree."

"They couldn't possibly mean this?" Jeremy said somewhat sarcastically, as he pulled one of the miniature Christmas trees out of his desk drawer.

"Oh, right." Sam blushed.

"What I want to know," Devon said, "is Carl's role in all of this."

"What do you mean?" Jeremy asked. "Isn't he part of the National Policy Institute, the far-right group that wants to destabilize governments and repress people of color?"

"Yes," Devon said, "but is Carl the leader? And what's with the train table in his garage? And why steal monuments and art work, why not ... I don't know, do something else?"

"He's in debt." Everyone stopped and gawked at Birdbrain.

22. Birdbrain's Reveal

"What?" Devon asked.

"He's in debt … to some people in that group," Birdbrain said matter-of-factly.

"How do you know that?" Sam asked.

"I overheard him talking to someone on the phone." In response to everyone's blank stares, she added, "In Paris. Remember when he grabbed me out of the air … on the Seine … after I stole the hat? Come on, you remember that, right?"

Devon found her voice first. "Yes, we remember. It's just … why didn't you say anything before now?"

Birdbrain ruffled her feathers. "I forgot about it until now."

"Okay," Jeremy cut in, "what else do you remember?"

"Just that he's in debt. He stole the art works hoping that he would be able to sell them later. Only, he didn't tell the others about that. He doesn't even really care about all that white supremacy stuff. He's just helping them as a way to pay off his debts. He helps destabilize the financial markets, they get rich and forgive his debts."

Everyone stared at Birdbrain. "What?" she asked.

"It's just that, that's a lot of information," Jeremy said. "You got all of that from a phone call?"

"Oh no," Birdbrain said. "He talks to himself, mutters a lot."

Sam grabbed H.D. from off the bed. "Hey, I was sleeping!"

"Yeah, well now you get to sleep downstairs," Sam said.

"What? Why?" H.D. complained.

"So, you can eavesdrop on our parents," Sam said.

"Hey, that's a great idea," Devon said.

"Yeah, but maybe not H.D.," Thing said.

"Why not?" Sam asked.

"Yeah, why not?" H.D. asked.

"Remember when you grabbed Carl's shirt when I asked you to get his hat?" Jeremy reminded him.

"So?" H.D. said.

"We need someone who can listen and bring back the correct information," Jeremy said.

"Oh." H.D. bowed his head and put his tail between his legs.

"Don't be sad, H.D." Birdbrain flew over and landed next to the dog. "We're all good at different things." She glared over at Thing as if to say, "Don't say a word."

Thing reached up to his face and pretended to zip his nonexistent lips.

Birdbrain continued. "You're the one who stopped the car. You're the one who scared Carl away. Let me do this."

H.D. nodded. "Okay." He still sounded dejected but his tail was no longer between his legs.

"Hey, why not me?" Thing asked.

"We need someone who can come back with facts, not commentary," Jeremy said.

"What's that supposed to mean?" Thing glared at Jeremy, clearly offended.

"We need to know what our parents said, without sarcasm, or jokes or backflips."

"Oh." Thing seemed lost in thought for a moment. "Where's the fun in that? Okay, you go Birdbrain."

"Do you mind, Devon?" Sam asked.

"Nope. But thanks for asking." Devon smiled.

"Ready, Birdbrain?" Sam asked.

With Birdbrain in his hand, Sam went downstairs and came up minutes later with a bag of chips. "I put her on the floor by the couch."

"Great." Jeremy grabbed the bag of chips out of Sam's hand and opened them. He grabbed some chips before passing the bag back to Sam. They ate in silence.

Sam spoke first. "Do you think Carl is going to try and get the trees back?"

"That wouldn't exactly help him pay off his debts," Jeremy said.

"They want to trap us," Devon said.

"What?" the boys chorused.

"They're trying to plan how to catch us and get the hat when we try and return the Christmas trees," Devon said.

"Then we shouldn't go," Sam said.

Jeremy stared at Sam.

"Remember what happened last time?" Sam said.

"No ... I mean, yes, I remember," Jeremy stammered. "But no, we shouldn't go. You're right."

"Have either of you ever seen the Christmas trees at Pier 39 or Union Square?" Devon asked.

Both boys shook their heads.

"Well, I've seen pictures, and they're really, really beautiful. It would be sad if they weren't there this year."

"But—" Sam started.

"We know they'll be waiting for us," Devon said. "And they don't know that we know that. So we just need to have a plan."

Devon stared from Jeremy to Sam and back again, but neither said anything.

The silence dragged on until Thing broke it, clapping his hands. "Well, that sounds like a great plan."

"We're thinking, Thing!" Jeremy said. He squinted, tilting his head. "Your arms are longer. How are your arms longer?"

"Oops," Thing said. He stopped clapping and his arms shortened.

"Wait a second," Jeremy said. "You can make your arms longer and shorter?"

Thing didn't answer, but his eyes went from side to side.

"You were doing jumping jacks the other day, and I couldn't figure out how you did it. How long have you been able to make your arms longer?"

Thing looked up at the ceiling. "Um, forever."

Sam busted out laughing. Devon grinned.

"Why did you keep it a secret?" Jeremy asked.

Thing looked off to the side.

"Thing?" Jeremy demanded.

"How else do you think I could have put Cheerios in the bottom of your bed? How'd you think I got my hands around the box?"

Sam rolled on the floor in hysterics.

"Do you believe this guy?" Jeremy said.

"Like I've said before, you two deserve each other," Devon said.

They laughed and joked for several minutes.

"Why can't we just do what we did at the Ferry Building?" Thing asked. "Go invisible, serve up some pizza and voila, mission accomplished."

"Because Carl will be expecting that," Jeremy said.

"So?" Sam asked.

Jeremy looked at him quizzically.

"Does it matter that he knows we can become invisible?" Sam said. "Doesn't make him able to see us, does it? He can't stop what he can't see."

"What about our parents not wanting us to go to the city?" Devon said.

"Wait. I'm confused," Sam said. "Weren't you the one who said we should return the trees?"

"Yes," Devon replied anxiously. She started twirling her hair. "I can want to return them but still be worried about how to do it, can't I?"

Stumped, the three friends sat in silence until deciding to give up. Jeremy opened his computer and checked YouTube for something to watch. He scrolled past a video of someone playing Minecraft to another doing tricks on a scooter. He continued scrolling until Thing said, "Stop."

"What?"

"Let's watch that."

"Which one?" Jeremy said. "Wait. The kittens? You like watching videos of kittens?"

"Well, all cats really," Thing said.

As Sam and Devon laughed, someone knocked on Jeremy's door.

"Yeah?" he called out.

The door opened and his mom popped her head into the room. "It's time to shut down this party. Sam, you're spending the night. Devon, your parents are ready to go."

Jeremy jumped up off his chair and walked toward his mom. He knew that she wouldn't appreciate it if he asked in front of Sam and Devon, putting her on the spot. "Mom, can I ask you something?"

"Sure." They both stepped out of the room.

"Can Devon spend the night? There's no school, and she has to go back to Portland on Saturday."

His mom studied Jeremy for a moment, thinking. "Sure. If it's okay with her parents. I don't see why not. Let me go ask."

As his mom went downstairs, Jeremy went back into the room and told the others what he'd asked. Within five minutes his mom returned. "Devon, your parents said you can stay, but they want you to come downstairs before they go."

Jeremy and Sam watched cat videos with Thing while waiting for Devon. She returned clutching Birdbrain. Jeremy's mom came with her. After laying the ground rules for the night—Jeremy would share the air mattress with Sam, and Devon would have his bed—giving Devon a toothbrush and reminding them to not stay up too late, she went back downstairs.

"Brilliant thinking, Jeremy," Devon said.

"Thanks," Jeremy said, shrugging her off. "Let's hear from Birdbrain."

"They're planning to all go into the city early tomorrow to meet Travis," Birdbrain said. "They still don't know what the code word "tree" means. Let's see…. They've contacted the authorities about a possible attack by far-right radicals. And they're trying to figure out how to make sure you all will stay out of trouble."

"Who, us?" Sam said, feigning innocence.

23. Risking Everything for Trees

"Okay, so we need to come up with our cover story for tomorrow," Devon said.

"We're having a movie marathon. I already said that," Jeremy said.

"And what are we watching?" Devon asked.

"Star Wars," Sam said.

"DC Marvel," Jeremy said at the same time.

Jeremy and Sam eyed each other before laughing.

"It can't be DC Marvel because my parents know I don't like those movies," Devon said. "Well, Captain Marvel is okay 'cause at least there's a strong female character. And I did like Black Panther."

Jeremy and Sam stared at her incredulously.

"She really likes nature documentaries," Birdbrain said.

"Don't look at me like that," Devon said.

"What about Star Wars?" Sam said.

"I like the ones with Rey, because—"

"Let me guess," Jeremy interrupted. "Another strong female character?"

"Well, yes."

Jeremy laughed. "Okay, then. Because having a nature documentary marathon isn't a strong cover story," Jeremy worked hard to contain his laughter, "how about action movies with strong female characters?"

The next morning, Jeremy heard footsteps on the stairs. Jeremy jumped off the air mattress before his mom reached his room. Meeting her in the hallway, he did his best to pretend to be tired and merely heading to the bathroom.

"Good morning, Jeremy."

"Hey, Mom."

"I have to head into the city for work. Devon's dad does too. Her mom and Cheryl are going to join us. Are you sure you'll be okay here?"

"Yeah, definitely. We were up late, and the others are still asleep." He then told her of their movie marathon plan. Working hard to not smile at the look of relief on her face, he nodded when she reminded him of the various food options in the house.

"I'll call to check in on you, okay?" she said.

"Sure. But can you call me on my cell? I might not hear the landline from up here."

"Yeah, sure." She gave him a kiss on the cheek before heading back downstairs.

When Jeremy returned to his room he found the others sitting up, waiting for him. According to their plan, they waited for Cheryl and Jess to leave, then knowing they couldn't be on the same BART train, took time to eat breakfast.

"Wait," Jeremy turned with concern to the others. "We don't have enough helmets."

"Relax," Sam said. "I brought one the other day and left it on the front porch." He peered out the front door. "The scooter's still there. Come on."

Using Jeremy's phone and Devon's dad's account to unlock the scooter, the three of them squeezed on, with Devon at the front, since she was the only one with riding experience. With a mischievous smile, she peered over her shoulder. "Ready?"

The boys nodded and Devon took off, faster than Jeremy anticipated. Sandwiched between the others, he struggled hard not to push Sam off the back. "Whoa, Devon! Maybe slow down a bit!"

Devon smiled over her shoulder, not letting off the accelerator. Jeremy reinforced his grip, and Sam did the same. Once at the BART station, they ditched the scooter. Noticing a train approaching, they ran through the turnstile, up the stairs and onto the train. Catching his breath, Jeremy caught sight of Devon half smiling to herself. When she met his gaze, he broke into a smile, and she, blushing, did the same. "That was some ride," Jeremy said.

"I love those scooters," Devon said, unbuckling her helmet.

"Obviously," Sam said, removing his helmet. "But maybe remember we've got more people on than we're supposed to, and take it a bit easy. I thought I was going to fly off the back a couple of times."

Devon's cheeks became a darker red. "Sorry. I'll slow down next time. But we did just catch this train. If I went any slower—"

"You did great, Devon," Jeremy said. "It was just a bit scary hanging on is all."

"Expeditious," Birdbrain said.

"Huh?" Sam said.

"Devon went really fast, speedy," Birdbrain paused, "expeditious."

Sam gawked at Birdbrain.

"Let's find some seats," Devon said.

They took the train to the Powell Street station near Union Square. Before they got off, Jeremy handed Thing to Devon. Since she would be the one to restore the trees to their original size, they decided it was most important that she not be caught. Thing would keep her invisible. She placed herself between the other two before disappearing.

"What do we do," Sam said from the back, "if we get separated?"

Jeremy turned around just in time to see Sam bump into an invisible Devon. He walked back to them.

"Let's meet up at the cable car turnaround," Devon said.

"Where's that?" Sam asked.

"Right there," said Devon.

"We can't see you, so if you're pointing, it's lost on us," Jeremy whispered.

"Look to your left."

The cable car turnaround was next to the BART exit.

They started to walk toward Union Square.

"Hold on," Jeremy said. "If we meet back at the turnaround, we'll be going the opposite direction from where we need to go to get to Pier 39."

"How about we don't get separated," Sam said.

"Not a plan," Jeremy replied.

"There's a Giants' Dugout store close to Union Square," Sam said. "We can meet there."

"What are you doing?" Jeremy asked Devon who had grabbed onto both him and Sam, making them all disappear.

"Our parents are right over there!" Devon hissed.

Jeremy looked around and sure enough, his mom, Cheryl and Devon's parents were standing across the square, near the temporary ice skating rink installed for the holidays. They seemed to be waiting for something. Jeremy saw his mom take out her phone. Devon pulled them behind a crowd of people and out of sight.

"Devon you have to let go of us," Jeremy said. "Thing can't keep this up for long."

Devon dropped his arm and Sam appeared on her other side.

"Where does the tree normally go?" Devon asked.

"Over there," Jeremy pointed. There was a circular area fenced off. He felt his phone buzz in his pocket.

"Hold on a sec," Jeremy said, as he pulled out his phone.

"Is everything okay?" his mom texted.

"Yep all good," he wrote back.

"How are you going to get through that without anyone noticing?" Sam said.

"I'm not sure," Devon said. "I wasn't counting on that."

"I can do it," Birdbrain said.

Jeremy glanced at his phone to make sure his mom didn't write anything else. Of course she did. "Make sure to eat something."

"I will." Jeremy put the phone back in his pocket.

"What?" Devon peered down at Birdbrain. "Oh, right. Of course. It's not too heavy?"

"I don't know. Let me try."

"There they are!" Jeremy heard someone yell behind him. He whipped around and saw two men running toward them.

"Devon, go!" Jeremy took off running, hoping the men would follow him. Sam was at his side as Jeremy caught a break at a light and ran across the street and into a department store filled with shoppers. Once inside, Jeremy looked back and saw the men glaring at him, apparently not brazen enough to follow them into the store. Over the man's shoulder, Jeremy could make out an odd-shaped object moving low overhead that he realized just before it dropped out of sight was Birdbrain with the miniature tree. Moments later, screams filled the air as the Christmas tree appeared at its full height, nearly five stories tall. The screams caught the attention of the men outside, who turned and ran back toward the square.

Jeremy nudged Sam. "Let's go. Where's the Dugout Store?"

"Follow me," Sam said. The two bolted out of the store, across the street and down Geary. People were gathering around the Christmas tree leaving the sidewalk mostly empty. Unfortunately that made them stand out. They just crossed the street, when they heard shouts behind them. Peering over his shoulder, Jeremy saw two different men pointing in their direction. Jeremy picked up his pace, and Sam kept up with him. They caught a break at the next light, running across on a yellow. Sam bolted into the Dugout Store packed with holiday shoppers. Jeremy scanned the store for Devon but couldn't see her.

"Do you think Devon's here yet?" Sam asked.

"Does she even know where it is?" Jeremy turned around in a circle. "Let's head to the back. She might still be using Thing to stay invisible."

24. The Chase

"Hey," a voice said from right in front of Jeremy.

Jeremy jumped. "Ahhhh!"

"Oh, sorry." Devon appeared, smiling.

"Don't do that!" Jeremy stammered.

"Oh, but it's so satisfying," Thing said as Devon handed him back to Jeremy.

"Guys, they're coming," Sam said, looking over his shoulder.

"Let's go out the back door!" The others followed Jeremy, but the door to the back of the store was locked.

"Hey, what are you doing?" an employee asked.

"Sorry. Wrong door." Jeremy turned to the others. "Over here, quick. Thing, I need you to buy us about thirty seconds. Can you do that?"

"How can I buy time?" Thing asked.

"It's just an expression. Can you make us invisible long enough for us to get to the front door?"

"Sure."

The three did their best to ease out of the store, but being invisible in a crowded space, they bumped into a lot of people.

"Jeremy, hurry up," Sam said from the back. "They've seen us somehow."

Jeremy glanced over his shoulder. They seemed to have made an invisible path through the crowd. And it hadn't gone unnoticed by the men; they were headed their way.

The kids bolted from the store, Jeremy releasing Thing to open the door.

"We can't outrun them forever," Devon said, chasing Jeremy.

"We don't have to. I have an idea. Follow me!" Jeremy yelled over his shoulder.

They ran across the street, turned right, went down a block and turned right again, ending back on Powell street. Jeremy stopped and waited for the others to catch up. "We need to jump onto the next cable car that goes by."

"Are you crazy?" Devon asked.

"You know he is." Thing climbed up Jeremy's leg and backflipped off, caught from hitting the ground by his carabiner.

"You were right. We can't outrun them. But a cable car can." As Jeremy said this a cable car came into view. "Now or never."

Devon took a deep breath and nodded.

Jeremy smiled. He ran forward and as the car came alongside, jumped on, in between two startled tourists who stepped away from him. Sam and Devon jumped into the newly opened space.

"Okay, that was scary," Devon said.

"It was sick!" Sam said.

All three of them looked back. The men had stopped running after them. Devon and Sam turned back to Jeremy, smiling. Jeremy, still watching the men, saw one of them pull out a cell phone. "Guys, they're making a call."

"We need to expect that someone will be waiting for us at Pier 39," Devon said wisely.

"Then we'll need to get off before then," Jeremy said.

A conductor approached them. "Do you have tickets?"

"No, sorry," Devon said. She pulled out some money and paid for three tickets.

Ten minutes later, at the top of Lombard street, they decided they were close enough and got off with several other tourists.

"Well, I've always wanted to see this street," Devon said.

"I've never been here," Sam said.

"Me neither," Jeremy echoed. "Well, shall we?"

The three hiked down the steep staircase, alternately commenting on the view of the San Francisco Bay and the cars negotiating the multiple, tight turns. It took them longer than expected to get to Pier

39 as they kept stopping to make sure they weren't being followed and pausing to peer around corners. When they were in sight of their destination, they stopped a final time to go over their plan.

"I'm just worried that they'll be expecting us," Devon said as she twirled her hair.

"Oh, I know they'll be expecting us," Jeremy responded.

"Right. And I'm afraid that they've thought up some trap to stop us," she added.

"Let us distract them," H.D. said.

"Even better, let's set up a trap for them," Sam said.

"What are you thinking?" Jeremy asked.

"We're guessing that they'll try and catch us, right?" Sam said. Both Jeremy and Devon nodded. "So what if Jeremy, you and I take off away from the area, and when they get close I'll set H.D. on them?"

"I like that idea," H.D. said, wagging his tail.

"And Devon, you replace the tree like last time."

"But I don't see an area cordoned off like there was at Union Square," she said, her finger now wound tightly in her hair.

"Oh, oh! Can I do my pizza trick again?" Thing bounced off Jeremy's leg in apparent glee.

Smiling, Jeremy nodded. "As many as you'd like."

"Weee." Thing did a backflip off Jeremy but misjudged due to his excitement and smashed his face into Jeremy's leg.

"Don't forget your other trick," Jeremy said as he unhooked Thing from his carabiner and handed him to Devon.

"Um, we might need that one sooner than later," Sam said. He stepped back from the corner of the building, his face clouded with concern. "Two men are walking this way, and I think I recognize one of them from the other day."

"Let's circle back, go around the blo—" The word stuck in Jeremy's throat. The men who chased them from Union Square were a block away, heading toward them. They couldn't go forward, but they couldn't go back either. And if they crossed the street they could be corralled against one of the buildings.

"Give me Thing," Jeremy said to Devon, holding out his hand. "And the hat." Jeremy was grateful that she trusted him and did what he asked, as there was no time to explain. "Sam, have H.D. hold those guys off." He indicated the men approaching from around the corner.

"Thing, make us disappear," Jeremy commanded. Invisible, Jeremy retraced his steps, running past the men who were now less than a block away from Devon and Sam. Once past them, he became visible once more.

"Hey, guys!" Jeremy yelled. "Looking for this?" He waved the hat over his head. Behind the men, H.D transformed, snarling, into a ferocious German Shepherd.

The men walked toward Jeremy who took off running. Half a block later, Jeremy glanced over his shoulder. Sure enough, the men were following him. "Ok, Thing. Now!" The men bounced off Thing's invisible wall, falling flat on their backs.

Jeremy doubled back to find H.D. snarling and nipping at the legs of the other men who were backed up against a wall. "Come on!" Jeremy said as he ran at and then past Devon and Sam who followed him.

As they neared the pier, H.D came bounding up behind them. "Devon, here!" Jeremy thrust the hat and Thing at her. Tourists crowded the area, some walking with intention while others milled about in groups, perhaps deciding where to go next.

"What worries me," Sam said as Devon disappeared from sight, "is why we haven't seen Carl." He reached down and picked up H.D. in his small, Basset Hound form.

Shouts of "Free pizza" rent the air as stacks of pizza boxes appeared on the sidewalk ahead of them.

Jeremy felt as if his stomach dropped to his feet. "He's here somewhere. Waiting. Sam, we're gonna need H.D., and we have to get to Devon." He took off running in the direction of the pizza, not waiting for Sam's response. As he neared the crowd swarming the pizza, the sixty foot tall Christmas tree appeared.

"Wait! Jeremy!" Sam caught hold of his arm to stop him. "If Devon's invisible, how can Carl possibly catch her?"

"You're going to lead me to her," said a voice that caused the hair on the back of Jeremy's head to stand up and goosebumps to break out on his arms.

25. Medallions and Stones

Carl grabbed Jeremy by the arm and poked him in the back. "Feel that?" Without waiting for an answer, Carl continued. "That's my insurance policy. You're going to give me what I want—"

H.D. interrupted Carl, barking and snarling before biting his pant leg.

"Get that dog off of me!" In trying to fight off H.D., Carl loosened his grip on Jeremy. Jeremy started to pull away but felt the blunt object push into his back again. "Oh no, you don't," Carl hissed.

"Sir, back away from that kid!" Carl spun himself and Jeremy around and came face to face with a police officer. In his focus on Jeremy, Carl forgot to pay attention to Sam who ran for help.

"I said, back away!" the officer repeated.

"I'm not doing anything," Carl said, stepping away from Jeremy.

Jeremy blurted, "He has a gun," as he ran to Sam's side.

The policeman unholstered his gun and pointed it at Carl. Carl put his gun on the ground and his hands in the air. As the officer arrested Carl, Devon appeared next to Sam. They watched as the policeman took Carl away.

"Um, we need to disappear," Jeremy said.

"Why?" Sam asked.

"'Cause if we give a police report, our parents will know we were out."

Devon handed Thing to Jeremy. "You and Sam use him until you're out of the area. Go that way." She pointed toward Pier 40, the opposite direction of their way back home. To his puzzled expression she only said, "I'll catch up in a minute. Just go."

Jeremy and Sam both held onto Thing and once they vanished, they hurried away from the area. Five minutes later they reached Aquatic Park, an area swimmers came to practice in open water. Several people were swimming back and forth, the black of their arms out of water revealing their wetsuits. When they were confident it was safe to do so, Sam let go of Thing and Jeremy hooked his buddy onto his carabiner. Soon after, Devon joined them.

"Why are we going this way?" Jeremy asked.

"We need to destroy and get rid of the hat." Devon pulled a pair of scissors out the backpack she'd been lugging around all day.

"You remembered the scissors ... wow." Sam shook his head. "You remember everything."

Devon smiled. "Not everything. But I do remember your idea of dropping the stones and medallions off the bridge, and I think it's a good idea after all."

"What made you change your mind?" Sam asked.

"Well, I don't see another way to make sure the pieces aren't found all together. I read that it's really deep under the bridge and with the ocean current, maybe they'll scatter." Devon glanced at a smiling Jeremy. "What?" she said. "I can change my mind, can't I?"

Jeremy laughed. "I didn't say anything."

"Yeah, but you were thinking something."

Jeremy smiled and merely shrugged.

Devon put the scissors to the hat.

"Wait!" Sam said.

Devon hesitated and looked at him questioningly.

"It's just that it's been pretty amazing having the hat and—" He stopped at the look Devon and Jeremy both gave him.

"If this falls into the wrong hands it could mean a lot of trouble," Jeremy said.

Sam sighed. "I know. But ..."

Jeremy eyed him quizzically.

"We didn't really eat lunch. Can we at least let Thing get us some pizza?"

Jeremy and Devon eyed each other, and they both shrugged.

"Sweet!" Thing said. "Drop it on me."

"Just one, Thing," Jeremy said.

"But make it a large," Sam said.

Devon laughed and put the hat over Thing.

They walked and ate their pizza, but after fifteen minutes it was clear they had a ways to go. "This is taking too long," Jeremy said. "Let's ride a scooter one more time." He indicated one just ahead of them.

"Sure," Devon said, "but first let's destroy the hat." She pulled out her scissors again. Jeremy and Sam nodded, though Sam did so reluctantly, and Devon cut the hat in two pieces. They stared at the pieces of cloth in her hand. They were just cloth.

"Well, that was dramatic," Sam said sarcastically.

"Maybe you need to cut them in fourths?" Jeremy's voice betrayed his uncertainty.

Devon handed one half to Jeremy while she cut the other, handed off the pieces to Sam, took the remaining half from Jeremy and repeated the process. Sam and Devon each held two pieces. The group stood, staring at the cut up hat.

"Ouch!" Sam and Devon echoed, both dropping their pieces onto the ground.

"It burned me!" Sam said, shaking his hands. Devon stared at the ground, and Jeremy followed her gaze. The pieces glowed red and then white, the colors emanating from the ground, into the air. A funnel of red and white changing to a deepest blue and yellow rose from the ground like a miniature tornado. The group stepped back. But there was no need. As quickly as the colors appeared and rose from the ground, they disappeared down into the earth. And where once there were four pieces of cloth there lay two stones and two medallions, the same pieces Devon and Jeremy hunted in Portugal.

After some hesitation, Devon bent down and touched one with her fingers. "They're not hot." She picked all of them up off the ground and put them in her backpack. "Let's get rid of these." They grabbed the scooter, and Jeremy pulled out his phone to use the app to unlock his scooter.

"Oh no," he groaned.

"What?" Sam and Devon said.

He turned his phone to face them.

"Ouch," Sam said.

"Six missed calls?" Devon said.

"I didn't have the ringer on. I am so done," Jeremy said. "I need to call Mom."

"Well, this is a predicament," Birdbrain quipped.

There would be no need to tell the others what his mom said. They could hear her loud and clear. "Jeremy! Where have you been?"

"Mom—"

"Why haven't you picked up your phone?"

"Mom—"

"I was about ready to leave work to come find you!"

"Mom! The ringer was off. I'm so sorry. We were ..." Jeremy hesitated. He didn't want to lie to his mom. But he also knew he couldn't tell her what they'd been doing. "I wasn't paying attention. I'm sorry." Jeremy held his breath, wincing, wondering how his mom would react.

A heavy moment of silence followed his explanation. "Can you tell me why," Jeremy could hear the anger in his mother's voice, "when you said you would be home watching movies, that you're in San Francisco near Crissy Field?"

Jeremy's eyes widened in shock. The others stared at him.

"GPS," Devon whispered.

Jeremy hung his head.

"I want you to turn around and head straight home. Got it?"

"Yes, Mom."

"We'll continue this conversation later."

"Okay. Mom, I'm sorry."

"I've got to go," she said. "I'll see you at home."

Jeremy hung up the phone feeling guilty and worried about what would happen when he got home. "I'll start walking back. She'll be watching my phone and will know if I go the wrong way. You guys go and get rid of those pieces."

"No," Sam said. "You two started this back in Portugal. You should be the ones to finish it."

"You sure?" Jeremy said.

Sam held out his hand for Jeremy's phone. "Sure."

"That's altruistic," Birdbrain said.

"Huh?" Jeremy glanced at Birdbrain before turning back to Sam. "Thanks." He handed him his phone after unlocking the scooter. "We'll come find you. Just stay on the Embarcadero."

"Good luck," Sam said.

"Thanks." Jeremy got on the scooter behind Devon, and they raced to the bridge. Devon navigated around tourists until they were several hundred feet onto the bridge. "This should do," Jeremy said in Devon's ear.

Once the scooter stopped, they both got off and turned to face the water. Devon took off her backpack, reached in and grabbed two medallions, handed them to Jeremy before retrieving the stones.

"Ready?" Devon said.

"Yep."

They both held their hands over the edge and dropped their contents into the air, to fall hundreds of feet into the bay below. Jeremy didn't know what made him do it. And he wouldn't have an explanation when confronted in the future as to why he didn't open his right hand but withdrew it from the side, slipping one medallion into his pocket.

26. Uncertain Future

"Ready?" Devon asked Jeremy. She looked at him curiously.

"What?"

"Nothing." Jeremy tried to arrange his face to not look guilty. "Yes, I'm ready. Let's go."

Devon eyed him curiously for a moment. Jeremy turned away toward the scooter and waited for Devon to join him. Devon got on without another word and drove them off the bridge, through Crissy Field, past Fisherman's Wharf and Pier 39, along the Embarcadero.

They caught up to Sam as he approached the Ferry Building. After hopping off the scooter and retrieving his phone from Sam, Jeremy exited out of the app. The three continued on foot the rest of the way to BART. Every once in a while, Jeremy fingered the medallion in his pocket, his mind trying to justify his actions. Was it simply a memento of their adventures as members of the Travelers

Detective Club? He tried to convince himself of that, for who knew if they would have any more adventures now that Carl was arrested and the other medallion and stones scattered at sea. But his conscience nagged him. However, they had more pressing matters to attend to.

"What are we going to tell our parents when we get back?" Jeremy asked the others. They spent the entire thirty minutes on BART discussing their options. After another scooter ride back to Jeremy's, they arrived to an empty house; their parents weren't back from the city yet.

"Jeremy," Devon said.

"Huh?"

"Call or text your mom that we're back," she said.

"She'll know. She's probably watching the GPS."

"True. But she'll appreciate you calling. Trust me."

"Okay, okay." Not wanting to hear the disappointment in his mom's voice sooner than he had to, he texted her.

Their parents arrived an hour later. Once home, the adults sat the kids down on the couch and issued a stern lecture on responsibility and accountability. Jeremy understood their reasoning. At the same time, he and the others had just saved the world from who knows what. How were they supposed to be in the TDC and follow all of their parents' rules?

No one complained about their punishment: Jeremy forfeited his phone and received double chores, Sam lost access to his Nintendo Switch, and Devon lost screen time, all for a month.

Afterwards, the three went upstairs to Jeremy's room. Jeremy flopped on his bed. Sam sat on the floor against the wall, and Devon stood looking out the window. Thing and Birdbrain started a staring contest, while H.D. chased his tail.

Jeremy fingered the medallion in his pocket. "Do you think that's the end?" He stared at the ceiling as he said it.

"What do you mean?" Devon asked.

Jeremy turned to look at her. "The TDC. Do you think that's the end?" Jeremy realized why he'd kept the medallion. He wanted a memento of his time in the club, if it were to be finished. But then he eyed Thing and realized that couldn't be the whole truth.

H.D. stopped spinning in a circle and froze, his tail in his mouth. Thing and Birdbrain broke off their attempts to make the other blink and turned, almost in slow motion, to stare at Jeremy instead. Sam looked up as well.

Devon left the window and sat down on the floor near the others. She didn't respond immediately. The room remained still, frozen like a picture. Then H.D dropped his tail, Birdbrain and Thing glanced at each other.

"I don't know," Devon said, shaking her head slightly.

"Oh, come on!" Thing exploded. "You were supposed to say 'of course not!'"

"I'm sorry, Thing," she said, "but I don't know."

"I don't think it's the end." H.D. sat on his haunches, giving off an air of confidence usually reserved for his German Shepherd form. His words drew the attention of everyone in the room. He paused for a moment, during which everyone stared at him, before he continued. "Where did we come from?" he asked Thing and Birdbrain.

"Beats me," Thing said, attempting a backflip from the floor. Unable to handle the seriousness of the moment, he also couldn't manage the flip from the ground. He crashed onto his back.

"What are you getting at, H.D.?" Birdbrain asked.

Devon started to smile as if she knew, but she waited for H.D. to answer.

"That large bird," H.D said.

"Who?" Thing asked from his position on the ground.

"The first magic buddy," H.D. answered.

"Baako," Devon said.

"What about him ... or her?" Jeremy asked.

"Oh, that guy ... or girl or ..." Thing said.

"Baako is the original magic buddy," H.D. repeated.

"So?"

"So," Devon said, "I'm pretty sure you aren't the first buddies to exist since Baako came into being. She most likely made others before you," Devon indicated the three buddies on the floor. "And that means there was a need for magic creatures before. And why would they suddenly not be needed again?"

"Oh, thank goodness," Thing said, and he turned to stare at Birdbrain again. The bird, apparently still interested in the conversation, ignored Thing. Thing poked her on the shoulder to try and get her attention. She wacked him on the head with her wing.

Devon continued. "The medallions and stones we found in Portugal—they weren't the first sign of magic." Jeremy just stared at her. "How did Pena Palace lose its colors?"

"No idea," Jeremy said.

"Exactly," Devon said. "It had to be—"

"Magic," Birdbrain finished.

Devon nodded. "And unless someone used the stones and medallions to take away the colors of Pena Palace, then scattered them over Portugal, there is more than one way to do magic."

"You're right." Jeremy felt the heaviness that led him to the bed lift, and he sat up smiling. "So, we wait."

Devon nodded.

"Fantastic, wonderful, absolutely marvelous," Birdbrain chirped.

Sam smiled. Jeremy and Devon laughed. Birdbrain, apparently fed up with Thing, took to rising to the ceiling and dive bombing him as he ran around the room. H.D. went back to chasing his tail.

Epilogue

On a Saturday one month later, Jeremy went down to breakfast and found his cell phone on the counter. *Yes.*

"Morning Jeremy."

"Morning Mom. So I get this back today?" he asked as he pushed the home button.

"For now."

Jeremy glanced up from his phone, which was dead, and saw a twinkle in his mom's eyes.

"For now." He gave her a smile which she returned.

"I need to go charge it." Jeremy bounded upstairs to his bedroom and plugged it in. He decided to wait to see if he had any messages. He'd told some buddies he was getting his phone back, and there were tentative plans to meet up at the skate park.

Four texts? That's weird.

He opened his messaging app. They were all from Travis.

"Jeremy. Please pass along my thanks to the others for a job well done. The three of you did a great job. I wish your parents could know. They would be so proud. I'll be in touch."

"Jeremy, did you get my last message? Just making sure."

"Jeremy, something has come up. Call me."

"Jeremy?"

ABOUT THE AUTHOR

While she works as a physical therapist, Sussi Voak rises before the sun to follow her writing dreams. This is her third children's book. Raised in the Santa Cruz Mountains, Sussi Voak recently moved from Oakland, CA and currently lives in Philadelphia with her son. Visit her author page at sussivoak.com to join her newsletter and get a free story.

Please consider writing a review on Amazon or Goodreads to help spread the word about this book. The Amazon link can be found at the very bottom of the product page for this book.

Made in the USA
Las Vegas, NV
26 December 2022

64208419R00122